CAN PIZZA ICE CREAM BE FAR BEHIND?

"What's for lunch, Mrs. Carlson?" Bonnie asked the next day.

"Well, we've got something different for you," said Mrs. Carlson in a cheerful voice.

"Great! I was afraid you'd say pizza again!" Bonnie reached out for the plate Mrs. Carlson was holding—and stared at it in amazement.

On the plate was a crispy brown blob that looked like nothing Bonnie had ever seen before. "What *is* this?" she asked.

"It's french-fried pizza, honey."

Look for these LUNCHROOM titles:

NIGHT OF A THOUSAND PIZZAS
Ann Hodgman

Illustrated by Roger Leyonmark

SPLASH™

A BERKLEY / SPLASH BOOK

For Leah Chapin

LUNCHROOM #1, NIGHT OF A THOUSAND PIZZAS,
is an original publication of The Berkley Publishing
Group. This work has never appeared before in book form.

A Berkley Book / published by arrangement with
General Licensing Company, Inc.

PRINTING HISTORY
Berkley edition/May 1990
Special Sales edition/November 1990

RL: 5.7

A BERKLEY BOOK® TM 757,375
Berkley Books are published by
The Berkley Publishing Group,
200 Madison Avenue, New York, New York 10016.
The name "BERKLEY" and the "B" logo are trademarks
belonging to Berkley Publishing Corporation.

PRINTED IN THE UNITED STATES OF AMERICA

Chapter One

Meet Your Lunchroom!

"Welcome to the new school year...and your new cafeteria!" said Mr. Haypence, the principal of Hollis Elementary School. "Isn't it just grand?" He paused importantly. "And I'd like you kids to know that this is more than just a lunchroom. It's the *future*."

"Oh, shut up," Bonnie Kirk, a sixth-grader, heard someone behind her mutter.

Mr. Haypence didn't hear it, though. He adjusted his glasses and smiled graciously out at the students assembled in the Hollis lunchroom as if he was waiting for something. Applause maybe? Bonnie wondered. Whatever it was, it didn't happen.

The first day of school at Hollis Elementary always meant two things: an all-school assembly in the morning, and pizza for lunch. At the assembly, everyone—from the tiny, scared

1

kindergartners to the big, bored sixth-graders—gathered to listen to Mr. Haypence describe all the wonderful changes that had
taken place in the school over the summer and
the wonderful plans he had for the new school
year. No one except the kindergartners ever
paid much attention during assembly—and
the kindergartners were too little to understand what was going on. Still, the first day of
school wouldn't have felt complete without Mr.
Haypence raving about *something*.

One year, Bonnie remembered, the assembly had been held outside so that everyone
could admire the new grass seed on the base-
ball diamond. Another year, Mr. Haypence
had sung his whole speech—in French—to cel-
ebrate that fact that the school had hired both
a new French teacher and a new music
teacher. And last year, when the school's new
playground had finally been finished, Mr.
Haypence had broken his collarbone trying to
give his speech while hanging upside down
from the jungle gym. Mr. Haypence liked to
make a big deal out of everything.

This year, of course, the assembly was in
Hollis Elementary's new lunchroom. After all,
it had taken more than two years to finish this
lunchroom—two years of eating lunch in the

basement and trying not to go deaf from all the drilling and hammering. It was the biggest and fanciest and most expensive lunchroom in the school district—in fact, in all of Pasadena. And naturally, Mr. Haypence couldn't resist the chance to give a speech on the brand-new stage—complete with electric-blue velvet curtains—that extended across one whole side of the room.

The electric-blue stage curtains matched the lunchroom's electric-blue walls. Bonnie couldn't help noticing that they clashed with the neon signs stuck up all over the walls— but then, neon isn't exactly supposed to blend in with its background.

Someone—Mr. Haypence, probably—had obviously had a lot of fun picking out those signs. "Place Trays Here," the neon sign over the tray slot proclaimed in blinking fuchsia. "No Pushing," the lime-green sign next to the drinking fountain reminded would-be drinkers. "Do Not Blow Straw Papers," warned the brassy yellow sign over the basket of straws at the milk counter. "No Coin Throwing," ordered the ice-blue sign next to the ornamental waterfall set into one wall. And in the exact middle of the ceiling, a fire-engine-red sign shrieked, *"PLEASE* DO NOT PUT FOOD IN

SPOONS AND SHOOT IT UP TO THE CEIL-ING!!!!!!!!" *They really had everything covered,* Bonnie thought.

The neon signs weren't the only decoration in the new lunchroom. There was the ornamental waterfall, of course, and, next to it, a row of gleaming new vending machines. The lunch tables—which had always been beige before this—were now made of crayon-bright plastic in primary colors. Potted palms were arranged gracefully in one corner of the room. And the grubby old linoleum floor had been replaced with gleaming rainbow tile.

The only thing the room seemed to be missing was chairs. Everyone was sitting on the floor except for the teachers, who were leaning against the wall.

"Are we going to be sitting on the floor all year?" Bonnie asked Bob Kelly, who was sitting next to her.

"I don't know," he answered. "Maybe Mr. Haypence ran out of money."

If Bob hadn't been a boy, Bonnie would have said he was her best friend. Maybe he was her best friend even though he *was* a boy. Bonnie and Bob had lived on the same block since they were babies, on a street about two blocks from school, and they'd never gotten out of the habit of walking to school together. Once in a while, they even ended sitting up next to each other at things like this assembly. Bonnie sometimes thought she and Bob hung around together so much because they were the only half-normal kids in Hollis Elementary School. . . .

"You don't really think they couldn't afford chairs, do you?" Tiffany Root asked with a little squeak of alarm. Bonnie liked Tiffany, but she had to agree with Bob, who called Tiffany the worrywartiest worrywart in the sixth grade. "We could get rheumatism sitting on this cold floor!" Tiffany went on. "Maybe I should have my mother call in and complain!"

"That's a good idea," said Bonnie gravely. "And maybe she could knit you a little rug or something."

Tiffany nodded. "At the very least," she murmured.

"Now let me show you a few of our new innovations," Mr. Haypence boomed into the microphone. He marched off the stage and up to a gigantic glass door on the opposite wall.

Mr. Haypence opened it with a flourish. Bonnie wanted to giggle. He looked just like the host on one of those game shows like *You Bet*

5

Your Life or *President for a Day*. "Our new walk-in microwave," he said proudly. "Big enough to hold three cafeteria workers." Some of the kids looked puzzled. "They just put the food on racks, of course. They don't *stay* in here," Mr. Haypence added quickly. "And this"—he walked over to a counter—"is our thirty-head milk-shake machine."

"Are we going to have *milk-shakes*?" a first-grader called out ecstatically.

Mr. Haypence paused. "Uh—well, someone else will be explaining about that later," he said. "And now, this gizmo here is the peanut butter spreader. It can spread delicious, nutritious peanut butter on *fifty* pieces of bread at a time. And these new drinking fountains here have hot water as well as cold, so you can make instant soup if you want. And *this* little beauty will open your milk cartons for you."

Bonnie shuddered as she eyed the milk-carton opener, a big shiny machine absolutely covered with sharp steel spikes. I think I'll just stick to the *regular* way of opening my cartons, she decided.

"Pretty impressive, isn't it?" Mr. Haypence went on. "But I bet you've noticed that one thing is missing from all this splendor."

"FOOD!" bellowed Rocky Latizano. Rocky

was another kid in Bonnie and Bob's class. He was well-known for having the biggest appetite in Pasadena. In second grade, he had once eaten the class guinea pig's food when his mother had forgotten to pack a morning snack in his lunchbox.

Mr. Haypence chuckled. "Of course there'll be food in here later today, Rocky—when it's lunchtime. But I'm talking about something even more important—the chairs you need to sit on while you're eating that food. I'm proud to say that Hollis Elementary—working with a well-known furniture designer *and doctor*— is going to be offering you the very first chairs designed to rest the neck while chewing. Researchers have discovered that *neck fatigue* is the main reason students feel sleepy after lunch."

"That's funny," Bonnie whispered to Bob. "I always thought it was because the classes after lunch are so boring."

"And I've prepared a special demonstration of this wonderful new invention for all of you this morning," Mr. Haypence went on. "Could someone please hit the lights?"

Someone switched off the overhead lights. Several of the kindergartners screamed in terror. "It's okay," Bonnie heard one of their teachers say soothingly. "We're just going to have a little demonstration, that's all. Kind of like a play! See the nice bright light shining on Mr. Haypence?"

It was a spotlight, and it was coming from a projection room near the ceiling. *Wow!* Bonnie thought. *We can watch movies in here, too!*

Shielding his eyes from the glare, Mr. Haypence called out, "Could you bring in the chair, please?"

Nothing happened.

"The *chair*, please!" repeated Mr. Haypence impatiently.

A door at the side of the stage opened, and in walked an embarrassed-looking man in a tuxedo. It was Mr. Skinner, the school's gym teacher. Bonnie noticed that he was wearing a red rose in his lapel.

What Mr. Skinner was carrying looked more like a torture device than a cafeteria chair. It had a padded seat, padded arms, and a padded neck rest with two padded metal prongs sticking out of it. Mr. Skinner slowly turned the chair from side to side so the audience could all admire it.

There was an uneasy murmur in the room, and one of the kindergartners started to cry.

"Isn't it a *beauty*?" asked Mr. Haypence. "And let me tell you right now, there are no other lunchroom chairs like this anywhere else in Pasadena. They're one of a kind! Here, let me just show you how it works."

With a big smile, he sat down carefully in the chair and slid his head into the two prongs on the neck rest. "You see, you just seat yourself in the ordinary fashion, and slip your head into these headholders. Sandwich, please!"

Mr. Skinner went out into the wings and returned holding a silver tray. On the tray was a plate with a bacon, lettuce, and tomato sandwich on it. He held out the tray, and Mr. Haypence reached for it cautiously. "Thanks!" he said. The chair was holding him so rigidly straight that it was hard for Mr. Haypence to move at all! He brought the sandwich stiffly to his lips and took a big bite. A slice of tomato slid out onto his lap. He ignored it.

"Delicious," he said in a muffled voice. "And you see, my neck is so well-supported that I'm not tired at all!"

"But Mr. Haypence, people's necks don't *get* tired when they eat!" someone called out.

Mr. Haypence smiled tolerantly. "Oh, I think you'll find that they *do*. Once you've tried this chair and seen how different it makes you feel you'll never look back. Now, let's say I'm a Hollis student, and I've finished my sandwich." He handed the sandwich back to Mr. Skinner. "Just watch: Well, I guess it's time for me to return to my studies," he said in a bright, fake-y voice. "I'll just get up from my comfortable chair here and—"

Mr. Haypence made a move as if to stand up, but his head stayed right where it was. "I'll just stand up," he repeated, struggling to free his head, "and return to my— Ouch!" He'd gotten up, but the chair had come up with him. Mr. Haypence quickly sat down again. "Mr. Skinner, I think this headholder is a little too tight. If you'd kindly adjust it . . ."

Some of the kindergartners giggled nervously.

Mr. Skinner bent down and studied the headholder. "There's no way to adjust it!" he said in a whisper that—thanks to the microphones—everyone heard.

"Well, just try to pull the headholders back or something, then!" Mr. Haypence hissed back. Mr. Skinner struggled helplessly with the prongs, but they wouldn't budge.

"We'll do it!" called out Larry Watson. Larry and his twin brother Louie, both sixth-graders, were known as the Human Demolition Team

to their friends. They sprang up onto the stage.

"No, don't touch it!" said Mr. Haypence quickly. "This chair cost a lot of money!"

But it was too late. Larry and Louie had each grabbed a prong. In unison, they yelled "KA-BOOM!" and yanked the prongs off the neck rest.

Mr. Haypence sat up slowly, rubbing the back of his head. "Thank you, boys," he said in a thoughtful voice. "You know, these chairs may need just a bit more work. Perhaps we'll just move in the old chairs for the time being. I'll have someone put them back after the assembly."

A whishing sound went through the whole lunchroom. It was the sound of four hundred sighs of relief.

Mr. Haypence walked back to the microphone. "You may take the chair away, Mr. Skinner," he said, "and change back into your street clothes. Now, does anyone have any questions about this exciting new facility?"

Jennifer Stevens, the prettiest girl in the sixth grade, raised her hand. "*This* year, will you let us have diet soda?" she asked.

Mr. Haypence shook his head. "Someone can explain about that in more detail later, but we've had this little discussion before, Jennifer. The administration at Hollis Elementary does not feel that diet soda's an appropriate beverage for youngsters."

"But it saves *calories*!" Jennifer whined.

"So does plain water—and since the new drinking fountain is filled with natural spring water, I'm sure you'll find it an excellent substitute," said Mr. Haypence smoothly. "Any other questions?"

"What's in the vending machines?" someone shouted out.

Mr. Haypence cast an uneasy glance at the gleaming new machines next to the ornamental waterfall. "Umm, various products," he said. "Someone will fill you in on that later. Is that it for the questions?"

Bonnie raised her hand. *"Yes,* Bonnie?" Mr. Haypence sighed mightily.

"Mr. Haypence, you keep talking about someone else explaining stuff. Do you mean our teachers?"

Mr. Haypence cleared his throat. "A . . . a very good question. I was, uh, just getting to that. When I say someone, I'm not *exactly* talking about your teachers—although of course I think it's always very important to talk to your teachers!" He gave a thin little laugh.

"No, I'm talking about a new addition to the

Hollis staff this year. An addition who has a lot of great new ideas about how to run this great new lunchroom. An addition who is well-trained in all facets of child nutrition, from lima beans to jellyb...*string* beans. An addition who will make sure each and every lunch you eat is *scientifically balanced* as well as delicious. I'd like you all to welcome your new addition—I mean, your new dietician, Ms. Weinstock."

Mr. Haypence began to clap his hands frantically. A small rustle of applause wafted out of the audience. Almost all of it was from the kindergartners.

Onto the stage walked the youngest, littlest teacher Bonnie had ever seen. She looked like a teenager. She couldn't have been much taller than five feet, and she had pale-blond hair, a pale-blue dress, and a pale, nervous face.

"Oh, my," Bonnie heard her new teacher, Mrs. Doubleday, say to another sixth-grade teacher. "So that's Alice Weinstock? I hear she just graduated from college last spring. This is her first job *ever*."

"Poor thing," Bonnie heard the other teacher say sympathetically.

Ms. Weinstock faced the stage, cleared her

throat, patted her hair, and cleared her throat again. Then she smiled tensely and spoke two words in a tiny voice.

"Health food," she said.

Chapter Two

Why No One Should Use Computers

"I KNEW IT!" bellowed Rocky Latizano. "You're going to poison us with a lot of grains and stuff, aren't you? Let me out of here. I'm going to barf!"

Mr. Haypence grabbed the microphone away from Ms. Weinstock. "Now, wait a minute, Rocky," he said warningly. "No one's trying to poison anyone. Just relax and hear Ms. Weinstock out."

"If he can hear her at all," Bob muttered to Bonnie.

It was true that Ms. Weinstock was talking awfully quietly. There was an eager smile on her face, but her lips seemed to be moving without making any sound. The lunchroom fell silent as everyone strained to catch her words.

"I'd like to welcome you to your new school,"

she said breathlessly. "I mean, I'd like to welcome me to my new job . . . I mean, welcome to the new schoolroom . . . or rather . . . *lunch*-room. I'm your new addition—I mean, dietician. And my job here is to organize the new menus." Ms. Weinstock sounded as if she wasn't quite sure she could manage it. "And I want to let you know how very much I'm looking forward to working here, and you know, how . . ."

Her voice trailed off, and there was a long, awkward pause. "Do any of you have any questions?" Ms. Weinstock finally asked in a shaky voice.

One of the kindergartners raised his hand. "Are you a lady or a little girl?" he asked.

Ms. Weinstock blushed prettily. "I'm a grown-up," she confessed shyly, "even though I know I'm not acting very much like one now. You see, this is the first time I've ever talked to a big group of people." She smiled down at the row of kindergartners in front of her. "If you'll all promise not to eat me, I'm sure I'll relax pretty soon."

"We promise," said all the kindergartners solemnly.

"She sounds nice," Bonnie said in an undertone to Bob, and he nodded.

Rocky Latizano started frantically waving his hand in the air. Ms. Weinstock scanned the rest of the lunchroom searching for other hands and pretending she didn't see Rocky's. Unfortunately for her, no one else had a question. "Uh, yes—what's your name, dear?" Ms. Weinstock finally asked.

"Rocky." He stood up with a swagger, looking around at his classmates. "About those words you said at the beginning. . . . You didn't mean all that stuff, did you? That was just because you were nervous, right?"

Ms. Weinstock winced. "Well, actually, Rocky, I'm afraid that I *did* mean them. You see, we're going to be trying a new approach here," she mumbled, looking down at her feet. "Maybe some of you have heard that cafeteria food—well, it isn't always very nutritious. Lots of—you know—fats and sugars and salt and caffeine, and other things that are bad for you."

"Give me *one good example*!" said Rocky.

"I can give you lots of good examples," said Ms. Weinstock. Her voice grew stronger now. "Cheeseburgers. French fries. Fried chicken. Chocolate pudding. I'm afraid most lunchroom food is nothing but thawed-out TV dinners. It's greasy, overprocessed—okay once in a while, but not the kind of thing you'd want to eat every day. Right?"

There was no answer. Four hundred pairs of eyes stared accusingly at the new dietician.

"What you're saying is, you're not going to serve any *real* food," said Rocky. "So what's left for us to eat? Worms?"

"Oh, no!" said Ms. Weinstock quickly. "There's plenty of stuff that's healthy *and* good-tasting. Fresh fruits and vegetables, whole grains, *healthy* milk shakes, maybe a little popcorn for special treats—"

"Hey, popcorn! That's good, anyway!" one kid called out.

"No butter or salt, of course," Ms. Weinstock added.

Everyone groaned, except Jennifer Stevens. "Salt makes my eyes puffy anyway," she said.

"So what *is* in the vending machines?" asked Rocky threateningly.

Ms. Weinstock brightened. "Well, that's a perfect example of what I'm talking about! This one"—she walked up to the first machine—"this one has fresh fruit, like apples and tangerines. This one has healthy snacks— crackers with peanut butter, trail mix. And this last one has vegetable juices. Carrot, tomato, parsley, and my favorite of all, Herbal Medley—"

Ms. Weinstock broke off. She must have sensed that no one was quite as excited about Herbal Medley as she was.

Rocky was staring at her as if she'd turned into an alien monster right before his eyes. "And what about the pizza we're supposed to have today?" he asked in a dangerously quiet voice. "You're not giving us steamed fish or some other weird garbage instead, are you?"

"Oh, no!" said Ms. Weinstock hastily. "I wouldn't dream of interfering with a Hollis tradition! As a matter of fact, I'm just about to program the mixing computer to make the dough and roll it out. Then I'll program the microwave computer to bake the crusts until they're half done. When the right time comes, the crusts will slide from the freezer into the oven and then onto some trays for their toppings. Then they'll go back into the oven again so the toppings get cooked. That way they'll be ready to eat when you come back here for lunch."

"And that reminds me," boomed Mr. Haypence suddenly, glancing at his watch. "We'd better cut this assembly short, or there won't be any morning left!" He gave Ms. Weinstock a hearty slap on the shoulder. She reeled backward, stumbled against the podium, then smiled politely and rubbed her shoulder. "Have you got that computer all figured out?" he asked her.

"Oh, yes," Ms. Weinstock answered. "I've read the manual very carefully. All I have to do is punch a few buttons. It won't be hard. . . ."

But she didn't look like she believed it.

Diego Lopez leaped to his feet. "Want me to do it?" he called out. Diego knew more about computers than anyone else in the school—teachers included.

"No, no," said Mr. Haypence. "Ms. Weinstock's our *expert!*"

Ms. Weinstock took a deep breath. "Well," she said bravely. "Here goes!" Then, slowly, she walked down the stage steps and, almost on tiptoe, headed across the room over to the microwave. She narrowed her eyes, reached out one finger, and gingerly pushed some buttons on the control panel.

"One . . . zero . . . zero," she said. "There!" she told Mr. Haypence. "That wasn't so hard!"

"Just one hundred?" Rocky Latizano screeched out in a scandalized voice. "But there are four hundred kids in this school!"

"Oh, but the pizzas are extra large," Ms. Weinstock assured him. "I promise you'll all get plenty."

She turned to the rest of the lunchroom. "One hundred pizzas are programmed to go into the oven at noon!"

"Okay, guys, let's try not to knock each other down," said Mrs. Doubleday wearily a couple of hours later. She had been trying in vain to calm down her class, but no one felt like learning a thing. They were too eager for lunch.

"I know you're all hungry, but that's no excuse for destroying the building." Mrs. Doubleday glared at Larry and Louie Watson. "That means you two especially."

The twins looked up at her innocently. "We *can't* destroy the building just by walking through the halls!" Larry protested.

"I'm not sure about that," Mrs. Doubleday responded. "It seems to me you've managed to make a good start already...." She glanced at the shards of glass lying on the counter where the goldfish tank had once been, and sighed. The goldfish were still darting nervously around their new home—a big plastic dishpan Mrs. Doubleday had borrowed from the janitor's closet.

"Don't worry, Mrs. Doubleday. I can probably get you a new fishtank for cheap!" said Junior Smith eagerly. "See, my dad can take me down to see this guy he knows. He sells glass, see, and—"

Mrs. Doubleday gave him an absentminded smile. Junior was a born deal-maker. "Well, we'll see," she said. "Thanks for the offer. Now, is everyone ready to go?" she asked. "Jennifer, put that mirror away. *And* the nail file." Reluctantly, Jennifer Stevens slid both items into her small heart-shaped purse.

"All right, then," said Mrs. Doubleday. "Enjoy your pizza, and I'll see you after recess."

With a whoop Rocky Latizano raced for the door. The Human Demolition Team was right behind him. On the way out, Louie crashed into Mrs. Doubleday's coatrack. Her coat fell on the floor. Larry slipped on it and accidentally broke the window in the classroom door. "Sorry, Mrs. Doubleday!" he said.

"Just go to lunch," she groaned.

"I don't know why people always get so excited about the first-day-of-school pizza," Bonnie said to Bob as the rest of the class filed out more slowly. "It tastes like wet leather with ketchup on it!"

"You mean you don't *like* wet leather with ketchup on it?" Bob asked in mock astonishment. "Maybe it'll be better this year, what with all that new equipment and everything."

"Maybe," Bonnie agreed. "On the other hand, it could be worse in ways we can't even imagine now. I mean, what if it has sprouts on it? Or little pieces of slimy mushroom, or something really awful like okra!"

"Oh." Bob's face clouded. "Health food! I forgot! Ms. Weinstock's kind of nice, though."

"She's totally nice," Bonnie agreed. "But I bet she won't last here for more than a week on the outside. Well, here we are. *Mmmmm* . . . I can smell that wet leather now!"

Ms. Weinstock was pacing back and forth in front of the huge microwave as everyone began pouring into the lunchroom. "Why don't you all take your trays and get in line?" she called out. "The pizzas will only take another couple of minutes!"

An avalanche of fifth- and sixth-graders thundered toward her.

"Stop *pushing*!" Bonnie shouted crossly to the Watson twins, who were right behind her. "What are you trying to do, trample everyone to death?"

"Calm down!" Ms. Weinstock was shouting. "There's no reason to get excited."

Once everyone was lined up, Ms. Weinstock glanced at her watch. "When you hear the buzzer, your pizza will be—"

BZZZZZZZZZZZZZZZZZZZZZZZZZ!

"—ready," she finished. "Okay, everyone! One hundred pizzas coming up!"

The lunch ladies picked up their oven mitts and stood at attention. The oven doors popped open. And the smell of school pizza—a smell somewhere between wet leather and burning rubber—filled the air.

As Bonnie picked up a tray and got into line, she got a good look at the new oven. It looked big enough to have baked a few school buses along with the revolving racks of pizzas that the lunch ladies were pulling out and slathering with tomato sauce and cheese.

Bonnie blinked. The lunch ladies looked awfully busy. They kept pulling out and slathering. And pulling out and slathering. And pulling out and—

One of the lunch ladies looked up. "Ms Weinstock," she called anxiously. "This seems like a lot more pizza than usual! Are you sure you programmed the oven right?"

Ms. Weinstock raced up to the front of the line. "Hey! No butting!" protested Rocky, who was—as always—first in line.

Ms. Weinstock ignored him. "Why, yes, of course I did!" she said. "I mean, all I had to do was punch a few buttons, and—"

She broke off. Now pizzas were spilling out of the oven faster than the lunch ladies could scoop them up. They were cascading onto the counters. They were piling up like plates. They would have slid onto the floor if the lunch ladies hadn't been there to catch them. And everyone could see that there were hundreds more still to come.

"Oh, dear," Tiffany Root moaned. "I hope we won't be buried alive in pizza bread!"

"Of course we won't," said Ms. Weinstock sharply. Biting her lip, she walked up to the computer.

"Can't you shut it off?" one of the lunch ladies called.

"I'm trying!" Ms. Weinstock squeaked. She wrung her hands and stared wildly.

Suddenly, Diego Lopez appeared at her side. "Let me look," he said. And this time Ms. Weinstock didn't protest.

Diego studied the control panel. Then he punched a few buttons himself. And a flashing red number appeared at the top of the panel:

1000—1000—1000—1000—1000—1000

"There's your problem," said Diego cheerfully. "You punched in for a *thousand* pizzas instead of a *hundred*."

Ms. Weinstock looked as if she was going to scream. "Well, make the computer stop baking them!"

Diego scanned the panel again. "It's too late," he said. "It won't turn off until all the pizzas are done."

Ms. Weinstock took a wavering step forward—and collapsed onto the ground.

Chapter Three

The Pizza Plague

"She's dead!" screamed Tiffany Root, staring down in horror at Ms. Weinstock's limp form. "You killed her, Diego! You scared her to death with your stupid computer talk!"

"Oh, no," said Junior Smith dolefully. "This is really serious. Her family will sue the school for sure. That'll wipe this place out. We'll have to have classes in some old moldy barn somewhere!"

"Okay, kids, out of the way," said Mrs. Carlson grimly.

Bonnie sighed with relief. Mrs. Carlson was everyone's favorite lunch lady. She always made chocolate cupcakes on holidays, and when the main course was something people liked, she made sure to give them extra-big helpings. With Mrs. Carlson in charge, everything would be okay.

Mrs. Carlson pushed her way through the crowd and knelt down beside Ms. Weinstock.

"I don't think you're supposed to touch a dead person," quavered Tiffany.

"She's not dead!" Mrs. Carlson said roundly. "She's only fainted! But we'd better get the school nurse in here. Diego, could you run down and fetch her?"

Diego darted toward the door. But just as he reached it, Ms. Weinstock's eyes fluttered open.

"No nurse!" she said weakly, struggling to sit up. "I'm fine!"

Diego looked back at her uncertainly.

"I'm fine," Ms. Weinstock repeated. "If one of you could just get me a glass of water—"

"We'll get it," said Larry and Louie Watson in unison. Before anyone could stop them, they sprang into action. Louie grabbed a glass from the counter, and the twins rushed toward the drinking fountain. Of course, it was just sheer bad luck that the full glass slipped out of Larry's hand on the way back. But at least the prospect of broken glass all over the lunchroom floor roused Ms. Weinstock enough to help her stagger to her feet.

And just in time, too.

"Ms. Weinstock, I see Mr. Haypence walking

down the hall," Diego reported from his spot by the door. "I think he's coming in here!"

"Oh, no!" Ms. Weinstock gasped. She turned to look at the huge microwave oven. It was still churning out pizzas the way a leaf blower churns out fallen leaves. Pizzas were piling up all over the place, and no one was even trying to do anything with them any longer.

"What if Mr. Haypence sees all these pizzas?" Ms. Weinstock babbled. "He'll . . . he'll . . ."

We've got to help her, Bonnie thought. It seemed a little weird to have to cover for a grown-up, but Bonnie could tell Ms. Weinstock was *not* going to be able to handle this on her own.

Bonnie squeezed her way to the front of the crowd. "Quick, everyone!" she cried. "Stand in front of the pizzas! Don't let Mr. Haypence see them!"

As one, the lunchroom full of kids rushed toward the stack of pizzas in front of the oven. Larry Watson accidentally stepped—hard— on Bonnie's toe, but for once she didn't mind. "Now, when he gets inside, *smile!*" she directed.

When Mr. Haypence walked through the lunchroom door, he was greeted by the sight of the fifth and sixth grades all neatly lined up with dazzling smiles on their faces, as if they were waiting for someone to take their picture.

"Why, hello, Mr. Haypence," said Ms. Weinstock shakily. "The pizzas are just fine, as you can see." Actually, from where Mr. Haypence was standing, the pizzas probably did look fine. But he could see only the tip of the pizza mountain.

"How nice," said Mr. Haypence after a second. "But why aren't people in their seats eating the pizzas?"

"Oh, we were just about to give Ms. Weinstock a formal welcome," Bonnie put in quickly.

Mr. Haypence beamed approvingly at her. "Well, isn't that wonderful! Mind if I listen in?"

"No, of course not!" Bonnie's voice sounded so false to her own ears that she could hardly believe Mr. Haypence didn't point his finger at her and shout, "You impostor!" "Uh, Bob was just about to say it," she said. "Weren't you, Bob?"

Bob's head shot up, and his eyes bored into Bonnie's. Bonnie suddenly had a vivid insight into the expression "If looks could kill."

"You owe me for this," he muttered under his breath. He cleared his throat for a long, long time, and then he began.

"Thank you for the pizza so spicy,
Thank you for the—the mineral water so icy.
Thank you for the first day of school,
Help us learn the Golden Rule."

"Thank you, indeed, Ms. Weinstock," said Mr. Haypence. "We're very lucky to have someone with your deep knowledge of food working at Hollis Elementary. Well, I've got to be off. I just wanted to see how things were going in here. New computer work okay?"

"Ten times better than I expected it to!"

"Good, good. Have a nice lunch!"

"Thank you," Ms. Weinstock said fervently when Mr. Haypence was safely out the door. "Thank you, all of you. I'll never forget this!"

"Hey, no problem!" said Rocky Latizano. "Can we eat now?"

Before Ms. Weinstock could answer, there was a thudding sound from the microwave oven. The oven door snapped open and discharged one last half-baked pizza crust. It landed with a thud on top of a huge heap of pizzas on the counter. Then, with a loud clicking sound, the microwave switched off.

"It's done," said Jennifer Stevens helpfully.

Ms. Weinstock looked around in dismay. There were pizzas everywhere. There were so many of them, they didn't even look like food. "Yes, Rocky, you can eat now," she said weakly. "In fact, you can eat as much as you want. But what am I going to do with the rest of these?"

"I'll help you stack them," said Diego promptly. "If we *all* help"—he glared at Rocky—"we can get them into the freezer in no time at all."

"Yes, but what will I do with them after that?" Ms. Weinstock wailed. "I can't throw them away. It's a waste of good food. Besides, where could I throw out almost a thousand pizzas?" She wrung her hands together. "Oh, I'm doomed! I just *know* Mr. Haypence will hear about this, and then..."

"Why don't you soak them until they get sort of melty, and then push them down the drain in the waterfall?" a third-grader suggested.

"Or you could let them dry up and lacquer them and use them for trays!" That was a fourth-grader.

"Grind them up for birdseed!" called out a smart-alecky second-grade boy.

"I've got it!" shouted Junior Smith. "I'll sell them for you! Let's see ... a dollar a slice—I'd get a quarter for each one for my commission—times one thousand ..." He pulled out a pocket calculator and began rapidly punching buttons.

Ms. Weinstock was looking more and more worried. "These are all excellent suggestions," she began, "but I'm not sure if they're quite right for—"

"Why don't you just keep serving them until they're gone?" Mrs. Carlson interrupted. "Then you can start bringing in your own menus."

Good old Mrs. Carlson, Bonnie thought. *Leave it to her to come up with a no-nonsense practical solution.*

A buzz of excitement spread through the crowd. "Hey, yeah!" someone said. "We could have pizza every day for the next ten years!"

Ms. Weinstock smiled gratefully at Mrs. Carlson. "That's a wonderful idea," she said. "But what about you? Won't you get bored serving pizza every day?"

"Believe me, I'd rather be serving pizza that kids love than stir-frying bean sprouts that no one will ever eat," said Mrs. Carlson.

"Well, okay, then," said Ms. Weinstock.

"We'll give it a try. You won't mind that, will you, kids?" she asked.

There was a huge burst of applause.

"Pizza every day!" shouted Rocky Latizano. "Fan-tas-tic!" He gave Ms. Weinstock a magnanimous smile. "I forgive you for Herbal Medley," he said.

Everyone agreed. Pizza every day was a great idea.

The joy lasted for exactly two days.

"What's the special of the day, Mrs. Carlson?" Bonnie asked without thinking on the third day of school.

"Honey, don't even ask," Mrs. Carlson said sadly. "You know what I'm going to tell you."

Bonnie swallowed. "Oh, right." Listlessly, she reached for the plate Mrs. Carlson was extending, then waved it aside. "I think I'll just have milk today," she said.

"What's for lunch, Mrs. Carlson?" Bonnie asked the next day.

"Well, we've got something different for you," said Mrs. Carlson in a cheerful voice.

"Great! I was afraid you'd say pizza again!" Bonnie reached out for the plate Mrs. Carlson was holding—and stared at it in amazement.

On the plate was a crispy brown blob that

looked like nothing Bonnie had ever seen before. "What *is* this?" she asked.

"It's french-fried pizza, honey."

The next day brought pizza cut into little strips and served cold on a bed of shredded lettuce.

"I can't take any more of this!" Bob fumed when he sat down at Bonnie's table. "Pizza *salad*? What's next? Pizza pudding?"

"It's disgusting," Jennifer Stevens agreed. "All this pizza is going to *ruin* my figure."

"*What* figure?" Bob muttered, but he said it so quietly that only Bonnie heard him. "We've got to do something," Bob went on. He raised his hand. "Ms. Weinstock!" he called.

Ms. Weinstock had been sitting alone at a table, studying a computer manual. She wafted over with a radiant smile on her face. "Hello, dears!" she said cheerfully. "Are you enjoying your lunches?"

"Oh, yes," Bonnie replied. "Pizza salad is a very unique—uh—presentation."

She felt Bob's astonished gaze on her face and looked down at her sneakers. *Why did I just say that?* she asked herself furiously. *I had a great chance to complain, and instead I totally lied! I guess I just can't say anything nasty to Ms. Weinstock when she's trying so hard and everything....*

"I'm so glad you're happy," said Ms. Weinstock. "You know, now I think these pizzas were a blessing in disguise. You all love them—and while you're finishing them, I'll have time to come up with some really special, healthy menus for you!"

"Uh, when will that be?" Bonnie asked. "I mean, how many pizzas are left?"

"Oh, *way* too many for me to count," said Ms. Weinstock with a laugh. "About seven hundred, I'd say."

"Seven hundred pizzas left?" Bonnie gasped. "We'll be eating them forever!"

"Isn't it terrific?" said Ms. Weinstock dreamily. She smiled at Bob. "Did you want me for something, dear?"

"I guess not," said Bob. "Bonnie asked my question."

"Well, then, I'll go back to my computer manual. I'm trying to learn how to program the peanut-butter spreader. Hey, I wonder how peanut butter goes with pizza!"

Before she noticed the looks of horror on the faces of everyone at the table, Ms. Weinstock turned and walked back to her table.

"The way she programs things, *we'll* be the ones who end up getting covered with peanut butter," Bob grouched.

"Oh, don't be so mean," Bonnie scolded him. "She's new!"

"She may be new, but this pizza is getting old. *Really* old," said Bob. "I'm just glad it's Friday—that's all I can say." He picked up his tray and stomped away from the table.

Bonnie stood, looking after him. *I wonder if I should try to talk to Ms. Weinstock,* she thought. *But I hate to hurt her feelings....*

She stared down at her plate of pizza salad. What little appetite she'd had before she sat down had completely disappeared. Guiltily, Bonnie sneaked her uneaten lunch into the garbage.

When she got home after school that afternoon, Bonnie was starving. "Hey, Mom," she called out. "What's for dinner? Boy, I can't wait!"

Her mother appeared at the top of the stairs, looking distracted. "Oh, hi, honey, Daddy and I aren't going to be here for supper. We're going to the Savlovs' house, remember? I just ordered a pizza for you."

Her mouth open and her stomach shrinking, Bonnie stared at her mother.

I'm fed up, she thought. *Fed up to here!*

First thing on Monday, I'm putting an end to the pizza plague.

Chapter Four

Dangerous Discussions

"Mom," Bonnie asked on Sunday afternoon, "what would you do if you really had to tell someone something they did that bothered you, but you were worried about hurting that person's feelings?"

Mrs. Kirk threw down the magazine she was reading and looked at her daughter with concern. "Why, baby, you can just go right ahead and *tell* me! I promise you my feelings won't be hurt! You know I believe it's *crucial* for mothers and their children always to be very open with one another!"

"But Mom—"

"So if I'm doing something that irritates you, just for heaven's sake tell me what it is! If I'm doing something wrong—and what you're saying tells me I am—then don't hold back! I can take it, no matter how bad it is!"

"But *Mom*—" Bonnie began despairingly.

"Go ahead! Don't pull any punches! I want my children to be *honest* with me! You think I'm a terrible mother." Mrs. Kirk's chin was trembling. "Well, I can live with that!" With shaking fingers, she pulled a tissue out of her purse. "Please, honey, share your feelings with me!" she said wetly. "Why are you mad at me? What have I done?"

"*Nothing*, Mom!" Bonnie shouted. "I'm not talking about you!" *Oh, why am I an only child?* she thought. *Why do I have to get all this stuff from Mom? Why can't it be spread out over some other kids?*

"You're not talking about me?" Mrs. Kirk's doubtful eyes appeared above her tissue. She paused for a second, then blew her nose energetically. "Well, that's a relief," she said in her normal voice. "I guess I just keep thinking you're turning into a teenager on me, Bonnie."

"Mom, believe me, even when I *am* a teenager, we're not going to have any big discussions about our emotions. Anyway, *I'm* talking about someone at school." Quickly, Bonnie filled her mother in on the pizza plague.

"That does sound a little tricky," Mrs. Kirk agreed. "Couldn't you ask Mrs. Doubleday what she thinks? After all, she's had a lot of experience at Hollis."

Bonnie grimaced. "I could, but then I'd feel as if I was finking on Ms. Weinstock."

"Then I'm afraid I don't see any way around simply telling Ms. Weinstock what you think."

"Oh," said Bonnie faintly. *Okay,* she thought, *I'll do it, but I won't do it alone. I bet Ms. Weinstock is even worse than Mom about criticism.*

"Um, I don't think Ms. Weinstock's in her office yet," Bonnie said nervously to Bob the next morning. "The light's off. Let's come back another time."

"Now, Bonnie, you know you can't even *see* Ms. Weinstock's office from here," Bob told her. "Come on. You can't back out now."

School didn't start for another half hour, but Bonnie found herself longing for the first bell. Why had she decided she had to have this little talk with Ms. Weinstock, anyway? And why had she persuaded Bob to come along with her?

If only he wasn't here, Bonnie thought, *I could have chickened out by now, and nobody would have known—*

"I don't even mind the pizza all that much," she found herself saying to Bob as they walked down the hall toward Ms. Weinstock's office. "Really, it's *great* the way the lunch ladies can

41

disguise it. Don't you think? You'd hardly even know you were eating—"

"Yes, you would," Bob broke in. "And don't you go giving Ms. Weinstock a lot of compliments about it, either." They were about ten feet away from the office now. "There's no sense in—"

Suddenly, Ms. Weinstock poked her head out of her door. "Did someone say compliments?" she asked cheerfully. "Hi, guys. Boy, I certainly could use a compliment. I've been here reading computer manuals since seven o'clock. It's already been a tough day, and the bell hasn't even rung yet."

Bonnie and Bob exchanged what Bonnie had once heard her mom describe as a pregnant look. "Well, we *are* coming to talk to you," Bonnie said. "But it's about the p—"

Ms. Weinstock cast a frightened look up and down the hall. "Don't say that word out loud!" she whispered. "Quick, come into my office!" Swiftly, she scooted them in and shut the door behind them.

Ms. Weinstock's office was—well, it was the perfect office for Ms. Weinstock. Hanging on the walls were dozens of framed poems written out in script. They had titles like: "Our Vegetable Friends," and "Oh, Lovely Bean

Sprout." The bookshelves were filled with cookbooks called things like *Smart Kids Eat Fiber, Fifty Tasty Sugar-free Desserts*, and *The Joy of Institutional Cooking*. Bonnie noticed that none of those books looked as though they'd gotten nearly as much attention as the copy of *You CAN Speak in Public!* that was lying on Ms. Weinstock's desk.

"Please sit down," Ms. Weinstock said. As Bonnie and Bob did, she whispered, "So . . . you want to talk about the . . . the . . . that food we've been having?"

Bonnie cleared her throat. "Yes," she said. "We just wanted to congratulate you on—"

Bob nudged her with his elbow. "Stick to the plan!" he muttered.

". . . to congratulate you . . . on how nice your office looks," Bonnie finished lamely. Bob glared at her. Bonnie swallowed. "But unfortunately, Ms. Weinstock, we're having a little problem with the"—she lowered her voice—"*pizzas.*"

Then, as politely as she could, she explained to Ms. Weinstock that the students of Hollis Elementary were tired of pizza, in any and all forms. And, in fact, it would be better if pizza were removed from the menu entirely, forever. Or at least until next year.

"Oh," said Ms. Weinstock. Her face crumpled. "I knew you must be getting tired of it," she wailed. "But I just hate to see good food go to waste—even though it's not actually that good *for* you! I don't want you guys to hate your lunches! But I also don't want to throw away hundreds of perfectly good pizzas!"

"Well, we don't want you to, either," Bonnie began helplessly. "That is, we *do,* but we understand that you can't. And no one wants you to get in trouble, but..."

"If we don't get something else to eat, there will be riots in the lunchroom," Bob finished for her. "And then you'll *really* be in trouble."

Ms. Weinstock drew a long, shaky breath. "I guess you're right," she said at last. "But what on earth can I do with all this leftover" —her voice sank to a whisper—"p-i-z-z-a?"

Bonnie could have sworn there were tears in her eyes. "Don't worry about that," she told Ms. Weinstock. "We'll take care of them for you. I've got a plan all figured out."

"You *do*? But you didn't say anything about—" Bob began.

"I'm just putting the finishing touches on my plan now," Bonnie interrupted. "I'll tell you all about it tomorrow."

"You're sure?" Ms. Weinstock said in a wobbly voice.

Bonnie leaned over and patted her on the shoulder. "I'm sure."

"What are you talking about? A plan?" Bob shouted crossly at Bonnie when they were safely out of hearing. "If a whole lunchroom of kids can't get rid of a thousand pizzas, what makes you think *you* can?"

"Well, I couldn't just let poor Ms. Weinstock worry like that!" Bonnie burst out. "Anyway, I'm sure I *can* come up with something. I know! We can have a meeting about it today during afternoon recess."

"Who's *we*?" Bob asked.

Bonnie smiled at him as sweetly as she could. "I'm putting you in charge of telling everyone in our class to be there," she said. "I just *know* you'll do a great job."

The Hollis Elementary School playground had been last year's summer project, and Mr. Haypence was just as proud of it as he was of the lunchroom. There were no neon signs in the playground, but just about everything else you could want *was* there. There was a water slide, a paddle-tennis court, a bumper-car arena, squash courts—you name it. The playground was huge, which was a good thing, because everyone in Mrs. Doubleday's class was there. They were all gathered around the jungle gym staring up at Bonnie and Bob, who were perched on top.

"So what's this stupid meeting about?" Rocky Latizano bellowed up to them. "Let's hurry it up. I'm hungry."

"Rocky," Bonnie protested. "You just ate lunch!"

"Oh, no, I didn't!" Rocky replied dolefully. "I couldn't stand to even look at that pizza. I mean, some things just stop *being* food after a while."

Bonnie was amazed. *I never realized he noticed what he put in his mouth as long as he could swallow it!* she thought. "I can understand how you feel," she said aloud. "That's why we called this meeting." Then she described what had happened in Ms. Weinstock's office.

The class didn't exactly start fizzing with ideas.

A minute of silence passed, two minutes—

"Oh, come on, you guys," Bonnie said. "We can't leave Ms. Weinstock hanging like this!"

"Why not?" asked Jennifer Stevens, tossing her hair over her shoulder. "She left *us* hanging with all these ten jillion pizzas, or whatever. If she's so worried about wasting food, why doesn't *she* eat them?"

"Why should we let her do that, when we could make a profit on the rest of the pizzas?" countered Junior Smith. "I still say *sell them*. We could store them in someone's basement and run a business out of our houses! People could call in to order them, then we could deliver them on our bikes, and maybe charge like, oh, fifteen dollars or so per pie. We could make some real money! Then we could invest in—"

"Hold on a second," Bonnie ordered. "That part about storing the pizzas in someone's basement . . . are they supposed to be in someone's freezer, or what? Because I don't think any of our parents have freezers that big even if they'd let us use them. . . ."

"Oh, we don't need to freeze them," Junior said easily. "We could just *stack* them."

"But they'd get all stale and moldy!" Bonnie protested.

"So what?" answered Junior. "No one expects kids to sell top-quality merchandise! Look at lemonade stands!"

Bonnie shook her head. "I don't think so," she said. "Moldy pizzas for fifteen dollars? Who else has an idea?"

Silence and more silence, broken by the donging sound of a volleyball ricocheting off the jungle gym. "We won!" a boy Bonnie didn't know shouted triumphantly as he dashed by the jungle gym and scooped up the volleyball.

"Winning," Diego Lopez said slowly. "I've got it! We could have a contest."

Everyone stared at him. "A contest?" Bob repeated.

"A contest," Diego re-repeated. "A pizza-making contest."

"Diego," Bonnie said patiently, "the problem is that we have *too* many pizzas, remember? We don't need to make any more."

"No, we'd use the pizzas we already have," Diego explained. "See, we'd announce this contest, and everyone who comes would get their own pizza to work with."

"Hey, yeah!" said Rocky Latizano. "*Custom* pizzas! And we'd get to eat all of them afterwards!"

"No, *they* would," said Diego.

Rocky's face fell for a moment. "Yeah, well. I'm tired of pizza anyway," he said.

"Of course, we could all be in the contest, too," Diego added. "We'd get all these toppings for people to choose from, and we could use them too!"

"But that would be—" Bob began.

"Hey, that's a good idea, Diego!" Junior in-

terrupted. "And we could charge admission—
big admission! Say, fifteen dollars apiece—"

"Junior, will you forget about all this fifteen-
dollars-apiece stuff?" Bonnie said. "I think it's
a good idea, though."

"Me, too!" Tiffany Root chimed in excitedly.
"And then when the contest's over, we could
have a really terrific party! I just hope we get
permission to *have* a contest," she added in a
worried voice. "And that enough people come
so that we won't be embarrassed."

"Well, I bet we can take care of the permission part by asking teachers to be the judges,"
said Bob. "If they say yes, that's half the battle.
We could have the contest right in the cafeteria, too, and cook the pizzas in the microwave. But there's one problem with—"

"This will be really great!" Larry Watson
interrupted. "Maybe you and I could work together, Lou."

Bonnie shuddered. *I can just picture what
the Human Demolition Team would come up
with,* she thought. *The world's first exploding
pizza!*

"Well, I'm going to make a really *beautiful*
pizza," Jennifer said dreamily. "With, like, little hearts and flowers and stuff, and maybe
some little ribbon trimming."

"Maybe you could give it a little manicure, too," Bonnie muttered. "Should we vote?" she asked in a louder voice. "All in favor of a pizza contest, raise your hand."

Twenty-five hands shot into the air. It was unanimous.

"Night of a Thousand Pizzas, coming up!" shouted Bonnie. "Thanks, everyone! I'll go tell Ms. Weinstock we've solved the problem! We'll start organizing this thing right away, and—"

"Just a minute, Bonnie," broke in Bob quietly. "I think it's a good idea, but I keep trying to say there's one thing we're going to have to figure out."

"What?"

"Well, say everyone's going to be making their own customized pizza. Where are we going to get the stuff to customize it with? Where are we even going to *find* toppings for a thousand pizzas? And once we find them, who's going to pay for them?"

Chapter Five

The Search for Toppings

A long, dismayed pause followed Bob's words.

"Maybe we can—uh—find some pizza toppings somehow," Bonnie ventured.

"Where?" asked Bob. "At the dump?"

"Oh, Bob, don't be such a grouch," Bonnie pleaded. She hated the thought of the Night of a Thousand Pizzas collapsing before it even got going. "I'm sure we can figure something out! Who's got an idea for how to get some toppings without having to pay for them?"

There was another pause. A long one.

"We could have a scavenger hunt," Tiffany finally suggested hesitantly. "Or pretend to have one, anyway. We could pretend pizza toppings was one of the things on our list and go around asking people to donate them...."

"That sounds like a lot of fun," Bob muttered sourly.

"Well, do you have a better idea?" Bonnie glared at him.

"Uh, no."

Neither did anyone else. Bonnie wasn't at all sure a scavenger hunt would work, but she felt it was her job to keep up everyone's spirits about the pizza contest. "I'll go along with you, Tiffany," she said. "Anyone else want to come?"

To her surprise, Jennifer raised her hand. "I plan to be a major movie actress someday," she said, "and this might help, you know, with role-playing and stuff like that."

Not that Jennifer showed much enthusiasm for playing a role two days later when the three girls set out on what Bonnie secretly called the Doomed Mission.

As they walked up the front path of the first house, Jennifer was still grumbling.

"This is a *great* way to spend a Saturday! Do you know I'm skipping my facial and my weekly manicure to be here with you? And all for some stupid pizza night that no one will even—"

"Shhh!" Bonnie hissed. She pushed the doorbell, and the three girls heard someone come thundering down the stairs.

"What if they call the police?" Tiffany quavered.

"You should have thought of that before," Bonnie whispered fiercely. "Now look partyish, everyone!"

The door opened, and the three girls found themselves staring up at a red-faced, panting woman in baby-blue sweats. A workout program was blaring in the background.

"I already . . . have . . . Girl Scout . . . cookies," the woman gasped, wiping her forehead.

"Oh, we're not selling Girl Scout cookies!" Tiffany assured her primly. "Because Girl Scouts should *always* wear their uniforms when they sell things, and—"

"GET those hips into the air!" squealed the television.

"Well, what do you want, then?" asked the woman. "Hurry! I've got to get back before they start the tummy tucks!"

"We . . . we're trying to collect pizza toppings for a scavenger hunt," said Bonnie. As she said the words, she realized how completely unconvincing they sounded.

"A scavenger hunt?" Now the woman looked faintly alarmed.

"Yeah. Like, you know, party fun—get it?" put in Jennifer. And she gave a totally fake-sounding laugh.

"Now, let's do some sit-ups!" shouted the

voice. "And a *one* and a *two* and a *three* and a—"

"Oh, no! They're starting the stomach exercises!" said the woman in a panic. "Wait here. I'll be right back." She raced away, leaving the three girls on the doorstep.

In a second she came running back with a tiny, flat tin. "This should help," she said, shoving it at Bonnie. "Bye!" She slammed the front door, and the three girls heard her thundering in the direction of the television.

Bonnie looked down at the tin. "Sardines," she said in disgust.

"Sure, I'll be glad to help!" said the woman at the next house they tried. "Just wait here." She closed the front door—and never came back.

"I don't approve of children eating between meals," growled the man at the next house, "especially *pizza*!"

"For a children's party, a quart of milk is the best thing I could give you!" chirped the old woman at the house after that.

And at the house after *that*, a little boy whose mother was drying her hair gave them a can of shortening and two oranges.

By the time Jennifer refused to walk any further, the three girls had collected less than half a bag of stuff. And—with the possible exception of the sardines, a slice of meat loaf, and a spray can of something called Instant Cheesium—they had nothing that could possibly work as a pizza topping. Unless you like pizza with Heath Bar crunch ice cream or pizza with instant cocoa or pickle relish or . . .

"I don't think a scavenger hunt is going to do the trick," Bonnie said disgustedly later that afternoon. She picked a soggy can of thawed orange juice concentrate out of the bag and tossed it into the sink. "We'll just have to think of something else."

"Bonnie," said Bob two days later during recess, "I think you'd better follow me and see what Larry and Louie are doing."

Bonnie did. What the Human Demolition Team was doing was glaring in unison at a tiny patch of ground by the creek that ran behind the school.

"Why won't this stupid stuff *grow*?" Larry shouted angrily, and stamped his foot.

"What are you trying to grow?" asked Bonnie.

"Mushrooms! Onions! Peppers! Tomatoes!" Louie yelled. "What *else* would we be trying to grow?"

"Yeah," added Larry.

"I...I don't know," said Bonnie. "What?"

"Well, what do you expect us to try? Sausage? Pepperoni? Meatballs?"

Both twins glared at her.

"Oh, I get it!" said Bonnie. "You guys are growing pizza toppings!"

"Yeah, trying to," said Larry. "But the stupid stuff won't grow! All we get is these little green things!" He pointed savagely at some fragile green shoots working their heads above the dirt.

"But Larry—and uh, Louie—that stuff *is* growing," Bonnie explained to the twins. Behind them, Bob was snickering into his elbow. Bonnie turned away so she wouldn't start giggling, too. "It takes a long time for plants to grow!" she continued. "In a month or two, those plants will probably start bearing. All except the mushrooms. I don't think you plant mushrooms the way you plant other—"

"A MONTH OR TWO!" Louie screamed. "We're not waiting any stupid month or two!"

Before Bonnie could stop him, he had leaped onto the patch of ground and trampled the fragile green shoots into the dirt.

Larry quickly joined in. Then he stopped. "You know, I've kind of been wanting to do that all along," he admitted sheepishly. "I feel much better now."

"Me, too!" said Louie. Whistling a cheerful tune, the Watson twins strolled away. Mission accomplished.

Bonnie sighed. "Well, there's another idea down the drain—not that it would have worked, anyway. Oh, Bob, maybe we should just give up."

"Well, I've got one more idea," said Bob slowly, "but I don't know if it will work. What about asking restaurants to donate stuff for the contest?"

"We already tried asking for food!" Bonnie reminded him. "We'll just get more crummy leftovers!"

"Not if we promise them free advertising," Bob said. "We could say that we'll make a poster listing all the donators—"

"Donors, you mean," said Bonnie.

"—all the donors, and put it up on the night of the contest. That's good publicity for them." Bob's mother worked in advertising, and she was always talking about how important publicity was.

"Bob! That's brilliant," Bonnie exclaimed. "That's the first good idea anyone's had yet! I bet you'll get tons of great donations! Boy, Bob, you've really saved our Night of a Thousand Pizzas. I'll always remember how great you—"

"Hold on," Bob said, looking at Bonnie warily. "What's all this *you* stuff? You're coming with me, or else I'm not going. And if I don't go—well, we can't exactly have a customize-your-pizza contest if all the pizzas are *exactly* the same...."

Bonnie sighed. "Of course I'll come, Bob," she said bravely. "It'll be...fun!"

"I said *pheasants*, you imbecile! Pheasants, not presents! Why would I want to roast fifty presents?" bellowed chef Jean-Claude Roche, the best French chef in Pasadena. Bob had decided they should start at the top.

"Well, I didn't *know* you wanted to roast them!" his assistant, a thin young man whose white hat kept toppling off his head, answered stubbornly. "I thought they were supposed to be little gifts for the staff! You know, morale boosters!"

"Gifts for the staff?" For a second, Bonnie thought Chef Roche was going to have a heart attack right there on the spot. "A staff like you deserves a *reward*?"

"Well, they're very nice presents," the assistant answered sulkily. "Some of them even have personalized monograms. You could at least save them for Christmas."

Chef Roche goggled at him. He opened his mouth and snapped it shut again. He turned red, then blue, then purple. Finally, he spoke. "You will return the little morale boosters," he said in a voice that had gone dangerously quiet. "And then you will order fifty pheasants from the market. Ph-ea-sants, do you understand? And after that, there are some potatoes back here than need peeling. Three bushels of potatoes, to be exact."

"They never treated me this way at Burger Bistro," the assistant muttered as he stalked toward the door. Just before he got there, his hat fell off and rolled under the butcher-block table. He didn't bother to pick it up.

Chef Roche stood staring after him. Then, with an inarticulate cry of rage, he snatched up the huge knife on the cutting board in front of him and pointed it straight at Bonnie's heart.

"And now," he growled, "what may I do for *you?*"

Chapter Six

Get Away from My Pizza!

"I can't believe he didn't kill you!" gasped Tiffany Root in amazement. "Do you have the glue?" She and Bonnie were making posters to announce The Night of a Thousand Pizzas, which everyone in Mrs. Doubleday's class was now calling Pizza Night.

"Here it is." Bonnie handed over the bottle of glue. "I thought he *was* going to kill me. If I hadn't started laughing, I don't know what he would have done."

"You started laughing?" Tiffany's mouth fell open. "Oh, Bonnie, how did you ever dare? I would have fainted away on the spot!"

"Well, it wasn't because I was brave," Bonnie told her regretfully. "I *always* get the giggles at the wrong time. Remember that movie *No Time for Tears*? I started laughing right at the part when Christopher tells Diana that he can't marry her because he has only two days to live."

"You *did*? I cried so hard I almost threw up! Wait, where's the masking tape?" said Tiffany. Bonnie handed it to her. "So anyway, you started laughing at the restaurant," Tiffany prompted her.

"And Chef Roche started laughing, too," Bonnie continued. "I could tell he meant to yell at us, but suddenly he just cracked up. Then he made us this unbelievable lunch. We had roast peasant—I mean pheasant—and these really great mashed potatoes...."

"And then what happened?" asked Tiffany.

"Oh," said Bonnie. "Chef Roche said he'd send us all the toppings we need one week from tonight."

"Well, I hope all the posters are done by then," Tiffany fretted. "Just look at this one! It's horrible!"

Bonnie knew Tiffany was only trying to get her to say the poster was good. Tiffany was always doing that. She'd say, "Isn't my shirt the most hideous color you've ever seen?" just so you'd tell her it looked great. Or she'd say her hair was worse than the Bride of Frankenstein's just so you'd tell her how nice it looked. Sometimes Bonnie got sick of it, and now was one of those times.

!!!!!NIGHT OF 1,000 PIZZAS!!!!!
THURSDAY, SEPTEMBER 15—6:30 P.M.
COME AND CUSTOMIZE YOUR OWN!
FUN FOR ALL AGES!
WIN VALUABLE PRIZES! PLUS EAT PIZZA!
WE HOPE YOU HAVE A GOOD TIME!

It was bordered with rows of what were supposed to be smiling pizzas. Actually, they looked more like moon-faced people with bad skin. (Really bad skin. The mushrooms were an especially unfortunate addition.) But Bonnie thought most people wouldn't notice them.

"It seems fine to me," she told Tiffany doubtfully, "except for that last line. Shouldn't we try to sound more confident than that?"

"But what if they don't have a good time? What if they have a really awful time? They'll think we tried to trick them into coming! They might *sue* us!"

Tiffany sounded so anxious that Bonnie decided to drop the subject. She had enough things to worry about herself without sending Tiffany off the deep end.

Bonnie called another meeting. The kids in Mrs. Doubleday's class decided that they'd bring their own toppings for their pizzas to the contest with them. Everyone else entering the contest could use the toppings donated by Chef Roche.

"It's not that unfair," Junior Smith insisted. "After all, we should have *some* kind of edge, since it's our idea and we're the ones who have to do all the work planning this thing."

"Besides, that way if he just donates a lot of French dressing or some lame glop like that, only the other people will have to use it," Rocky Latizano put in.

"Yeah," said Larry. "We want our recipes to be *ace!*"

"He's right," said Louie. "We don't want to take any chances with some weird stuff that crazy chef gives us...."

So everyone in the class started making pizzas from scratch at home, trying to come up with combinations that no one else would think of. And everyone was convinced they would create the greatest new pizza the world had ever seen—a pizza like no other!

Since Bonnie was in charge of Pizza Night, every person in the class kept asking her to come home with them after school to taste their fabulous, original recipe!

"Squid and goat cheese? How...how different!" Bonnie told Miranda Pei one afternoon.

She looked down at the slimy white rings of raw squid on the Peis' kitchen counter and did her best not to shudder.

"Well, I don't really like squid," Miranda confessed. She pulled on a pair of rubber gloves and gingerly began scattering the squid rings across the surface of the pizza. "Or goat cheese. That's why I asked you to taste-test it for me. That way, you can tell me what you think the judges will say." Miranda slid the squidded-up pizza into the oven and set the timer for fifteen minutes.

Usually, time passes slowly if you're watching the second hand go around. But for Bonnie, with the prospect of that squid staring her in the mouth, fifteen minutes had never raced by so fast.

"Okay, it's done!" Miranda chirped long before Bonnie had been able to come to grips with the new taste sensation she was about to experience. She watched apprehensively as Miranda cut a huge wedge, put it on a plate, and handed it to her with a flourish.

"How is it?" she asked Bonnie eagerly.

Bonnie didn't answer. She was thinking, *I wonder if the problem is that I'm chewing. Maybe if I just hold my mouth still and let this piece dissolve ...*

She waited, but nothing happened. At last, she settled for chewing the pizza rapidly with her front teeth, like a squirrel. But no matter what she did, nothing could disguise the fact that it tasted the way a dog's breath starts to smell when he's getting old.

"Uhh, could I have a glass of water?" she mumbled. Miranda handed her one. Bonnie forced herself to swallow.

"Well?" Miranda asked eagerly.

"Mmmmm—really weird," Bonnie said at last. "I mean, really fascinating.... Such unique flavors! That chopped pickle seems too ... surprising, though. I think it, ummm, sort of clashes a little with the other stuff."

"Oh, thanks, Bonnie," said Miranda happily. "I'll try artichoke hearts instead."

Squid/goat cheese/pickle was only one in a long line of pizzas that should never have been invented. Bonnie also gagged down samples of a dessert pizza topped with brown sugar, honey, coconut, banana, and dotted all over with strawberry jam; pizza rolled up around a strip of liverwurst; and a truly amazing pizza topped with fried chicken, crumbled bacon, fried eggs, and crushed potato chips. That particular one was Rocky Latizano's invention, and he was amazed when Bonnie couldn't finish the sample he offered her.

"Not enough salt?" he asked anxiously.

"No ... the salt's perfect," Bonnie gasped.

"Too bland?" Rocky asked.

"NO! I mean it's fine."

"Then what's the matter with it?" Rocky demanded sounding genuinely bewildered.

"Rocky, it's the *grease!*" Just those couple of bites had made Bonnie feel completely waterproof.

Rocky didn't seem worried. "Well, it's really a cold-weather pizza," he said. "In winter, people's appetites are bigger. You know, they need more fat. I'll make sure to tell the judges that."

If that first bite doesn't give them all heart attacks, Bonnie thought. She decided she'd better make sure she found judges who were in good shape.

"I think Pizza Night is getting to me," Bonnie gasped to Bob the next day as they lined up for lunch. "I don't feel very hungry somehow." She still hadn't gotten over the effects of all her pizza taste-testing.

"At least Ms. Weinstock looks happy," Bob said.

It was true. Now that she knew the pizzas

were going to be taken care of, Ms. Weinstock was positively beaming. When she saw Bob and Bonnie in line, she came running over.

"Hi, Ms. Weinstock!" Bonnie said.

"What's for lunch today?" Bob asked.

"You're going to love it!" Ms. Weinstock gushed. "And it's so good for you, too. So much better than that horrible pizza . . . "

"But what is it?" Bob asked again. Bonnie thought he sounded a little nervous.

"Zucchini–brussels sprouts soup, and tofu burgers with lima beans!" Ms. Weinstock answered brightly. "It's fulfills *all* your nutritional requirements—fiber, calcium, protein, and—"

"Uhhh, it sounds great, Ms. Weinstock," Bob mumbled. "Really yummy, but . . . uhhh . . . I'm not all that hungry, so—"

"Me either, " Bonnie put in quickly. "All that eating I'm doing for Pizza Night, you know?"

And leaving a bewildered-looking Ms. Weinstock standing next to her zucchini–brussels sprouts soup, Bob and Bonnie left the lunchroom in a hurry.

"We have to do something!" Bob hissed as they walked down the hall toward the door to the playground. "That stuff almost makes me wish we were still eating pizza!"

"I know," Bonnie replied glumly. "But listen, Bob, we *have* to take care of the pizza plague first. Then we can tackle the—"

"Health-food horror?" Bob finished for her.

Bonnie nodded grimly.

"What is going on here?" Mrs. Doubleday asked during the afternoon three days before the contest. She frowned down at Jonathan Matterhorn. "Why are you holding your arms that way?"

Jonathan was crouched down low over his desk, his arms folded around a pile of papers as if he was afraid someone was going to sneak up and tear them out of his hands at any moment.

"We're not having a test today," Mrs. Doubleday continued. "At least as far as *I* know. So I don't think there's any reason to guard your work *quite* so carefully. Unless you know something I don't?"

"No, Mrs. Doubleday," Jonathan replied. "I'm just making sure no one sees my recipes for Pizza Night."

"Copyright them!" Junior Smith called out. "That's what I did with mine. My father introduced me to this lawyer, and he said that you should copyright any original invention. That way—"

"I am *not* interested in what a lawyer told you *or* your father," said Mrs. Doubleday in an icy voice. "What I *am* interested in is the way no one in this class trusts anyone *else* in this class. Ever since you decided to sponsor Pizza Night, each and every one of you is acting as though your neighbor's about to stab you in the back!"

Bonnie bit her lip. *That's not fair*, she thought. I'm *not acting like that. I haven't even come up with an idea for my pizza yet!*

"Come on, guys!" Mrs. Doubleday pleaded. "It's just a pizza contest. You're not being chosen to run the world!"

Bonnie glanced around the room. Nobody looked convinced by Mrs. Doubleday's words.

"Okay?" their teacher asked. "Good. Let's stop worrying about pizza-recipe theft and have a little fun."

Suddenly she broke off. "What is it, Kelly?" she asked. Kelly Sills was waving her hand frantically in the air. "Do you have a question?"

"Which do you think would go better with sliced hot dogs and Velveeta—mustard or ketchup?" Kelly said. She glared at the rest of the kids in the class. "*Not* that I'm planning to use any of that stuff on my pizza, so don't anybody go getting ideas."

Mrs. Doubleday sighed. "It's nice to know my little speech made such a big impression," she said.

"Mrs. Doubleday's right," Bonnie commented as she and Bob walked home from school that afternoon. "People *are* going overboard about this contest. It's really kind of silly, don't you think?"

"Completely stupid," he agreed. "I heard Junior Smith telling the Watson twins he'd call his lawyer if he saw them anywhere *near* his house. Then the twins said *they* were going to get their own lawyer. You'd think no one had anything better to do than go around stealing recipes. Have you decided what your topping's going to be yet?"

"I thought about it some more while Mrs. Doubleday was yelling at us," Bonnie said slowly, "and I think I've finally come up with a good idea. You know, all the pizzas I've tasted so far have been so weird that I started wondering—why not do a plain old regular-style pizza? The judges won't see very many of those!

"So what I'll do is make this really great tomato sauce by hand, and then go to an Italian grocery store and buy some really excellent mozzarella and some great big mushrooms, and then I'll call it 'Bonnie's Italian Classic,' and—Bob, why are you staring at me like that?"

"You're kidding, aren't you?"

"Why would I be kidding? It's not funny enough to kid about! I mean, if I'd told you I was doing a sweet-potato pizza with sushi on top, you'd have—"

"But *I'm* doing a traditional pizza," Bob told her. "I made the sauce last night. It's going to have mozzarella, mushrooms, and sausage."

"Well, that's okay, then," said Bonnie. "Mine doesn't have sausage, so they won't be too much alike. What a relief! I'd hate to have to come up with something diff—"

"I think they *will* be too much alike," Bob interrupted her. "And I've already started on mine. Would you mind changing your idea?"

"Why should I?" Bonnie demanded. "It's just a coincidence that we both came up with practically the same pizza. I didn't copy you!"

"The judges won't know that," Bob pointed out. "And what if they try your pizza before mine? They'll think *I* copied *you!*"

"But I *can't* come up with something else!" Bonnie wailed. "It took me so much longer than anyone else to come up *this* stupid idea!"

"Well, if you think it's so stupid, then you *really* shouldn't mind changing."

"Well, I'm not going to," Bonnie snapped back. "Pizza Night was my idea, not yours."

"It was not!" Bob was practically yelling. "It was Diego's idea, and you know it!"

"He had the idea about the contest, but I'm the one who had the idea to help Ms. Weinstock," Bonnie said loftily. "And I don't think all this childish squabbling will help her one bit."

"Well, I'm the one who figured out where to get the toppings!" Bob shot back.

"*Great*," Bonnie said sarcastically. "And you almost got us murdered doing it!"

"That's the most ridiculous thing I ever heard." Bob really looked mad now. "So you're not going to change your pizza?" he asked.

"Nope."

"Fine. Then you can just forget about me helping you any more with this stupid contest. I hope you don't find any judges. I hope no one comes to Pizza Night. And I hope your pizza blows up in your face!"

And before Bonnie could answer, Bob stomped off down the street.

Bonnie's first reaction to Bob's departure was not very noble.

Now I'll have to find the judges all by myself! she thought. *And Bob knows I was counting on asking him to help me!*

"Wait. I'll change my pizza after all!" she called after him. Then she stopped.

Bob is too smart to believe I'd change my mind this easily, she told herself. *He'll guess I'm trying to get him to help me, and if I mention the judges again, he'll know for sure. Oh, why did I put off finding judges until so late?*

Chapter Seven
The Chef's Surprise

The next morning, Bonnie looked down at her list of possible judges and took a deep breath. She'd narrowed it down to three first choices and nine second choices. The first three on her list were the teachers she was least afraid of. That was because they were all pretty weird—too weird to be scary. Bonnie took a deep breath and walked down the hall to see the first person on her list, Mrs. Dowdy, the home-economics teacher.

Mrs. Dowdy was famous around school for making *all* her clothes—underwear included. No one ever saw her without some sewing project in her hand. She stored knitting needles behind her ear, like pencils. As she walked through the halls, she scattered bits of yarn and scraps of fabric around her.

When Bonnie walked into her classroom,

Mrs. Dowdy was busily hemming a long, weird, gray dress-type thing. Bonnie quickly looked away. Whatever it was, it was disgusting-looking.

"I'm making a nice wool slip for winter," Mrs. Dowdy said brightly. "Have you come to sign up for the Bedroom Slipper Workshop?"

"No, not exactly," Bonnie said. "I was ummm, well, wondering whether you'd be one of the judges for uhh, Pizza Night. See, we're having this big contest, and—"

Mrs. Dowdy's lips became a tight line. "I know *all* about it," she snapped. "Taking time away from your classes to eat horrible pizza. I've seen you kids cluttering up our nice clean halls with posters. Pizza Night, huh? More like Pizza Disaster, in my opinion. You know what will happen, don't you? Strangers will come into our school tramping mud all over the place and eating that...I can't even bear to say it. Why, the school will look like a junkyard when your Pizza Night is over! And just *who* is going to clean it up, may I ask?"

Mrs. Dowdy was really worked up now. She yanked a pin out of her collar and jabbed it viciously into the gray slip.

"Mrs. Dowdy, I really don't think it will be that much of a problem!" Bonnie said. "We have a very dedicated cleanup committee. And anyway," she added, "we thought that someone with all your ... your domestic experience would make a much better judge than ... than someone younger who wouldn't know nearly as much as I'm sure you do about pizza."

It was the perfect touch. Mrs. Dowdy actually put down the gray slip and smiled.

"Well, *that is* certainly true. Hmmm ... Let me think for a minute. All right, Bonnie, I'll be one of the judges. Oh, what fun! I'll start making my judge's robe right away."

"Will you have time?" Bonnie asked. "Pizza Night is the day after tomorrow!"

"Oh, I'll stay up all night if need be. Let's see, I can weave some black cloth on my Porta-Loom ..."

Bonnie left Mrs. Dowdy happily making plans. Her next stop was Mr. Windle's office. Mr. Windle was a rumpled-looking, bespectacled old man. He taught social studies, and *he* was famous for never finishing his sentences.

Mr. Windle said he'd be glad to be a judge. At least that's what he *seemed* to be saying. . . .

"Why, I think a pizza contest would be most ..." he mumbled. "Assuming, of course, that the pizza tastes ... But I guess the fun of these things is partly the fact that ...

Although I haven't had a pizza in twenty-five ... My wife doesn't like spicy ... But pepperoni is one of my ... Thank you for ..."

Bonnie just nodded. "Thanks, Mr. Windle!" she said.

Mr. Windle shut his mouth with a snap and smiled vaguely in Bonnie's general direction.

"We'll see you on Thursday night, then," she said.

"I'll be looking forward to ..." Mr. Windle replied.

Bonnie had saved what she guessed would be the easiest person until last—Mrs. Carlson, the lunch lady who had helped Ms. Weinstock out of her faint on the first day of school. Mrs. Carlson, too, agreed to be a judge right away.

"I'm only too delighted to do anything I can to help that poor child in her job," she said robustly. "When I think how nervous I was *my* first year in this jungle ... Well, honey, you can definitely count me in."

With the Judge Problem taken care of, Bonnie turned her attention to the Setting Up the Night Before Problem. Tiffany and Jennifer were already helping, but Bonnie was sure they'd need another person. There was no point in asking Bob for his help. Every time he saw Bonnie, he made awful faces that made him look as if he were about to be sick. Naturally, Bonnie had been walking to and from school alone. The one time she and Bob had actually found themselves on the same block, Bob had crossed to the other side of the street.

So Bonnie decided to ask Diego Lopez instead.

"Sure, I'll be glad to help," Diego said instantly. "What do we have to do?"

"Not much," Bonnie assured him. "Just decorate the lunchroom, set up tables for the judges—things like that."

"Should I bring my tool set?" Diego asked eagerly. "Maybe we could do some construction? I could build sort of a platform for the winners to stand on, like in the Olympics. And what about some kind of dunking booth for the losers? Whoever the judges said had made the *worst* pizza would be strapped into this little seat, and we could dunk him in a big vat of tomato sauce! And—"

"That's okay," Bonnie broke in hastily. "I don't think we need to do any *major* construction. But you could bring your tool set just in case," she added when she saw how disappointed Diego looked. "We'll meet at the front door at six tomorrow night. Ms. Weinstock's coming to help, too, and she'll unlock the door for us."

* * *

Bonnie had two hours to go before she was supposed to meet Diego and Ms. Weinstock at school, and she just couldn't seem to settle down. She was in the kitchen at home, pacing. Back and forth she marched.

Up to one end of the kitchen. "No, I'm *not* going to change my pizza topping!" she vowed. "I don't *care* how mad Bob gets! It was just as much my idea as his!"

Back to the other end. "On the other hand, I'm kind of in charge of Pizza Night. Doesn't it seem kind of childish of me to be so stubborn?"

Up to the other end again. "But Bob was so horrible about this!" she told herself. "A real friend wouldn't make such a fuss about some dumb old pizza recipe. Anyhow, I bet there will be lots of duplicates. How many different kinds of pizza can there be?"

And back to the other end. "But it's horrible to have anyone mad at me, especially Bob!"

The truth was, life wasn't too much fun without a best friend!

Suddenly, Bonnie stopped pacing.

"Okay, okay...I'll change my pizza," she said out loud.

Then she flung open the refrigerator door. She peered into the crisper. There was:

1. half a head of brown-edged iceberg lettuce

2. a withered carrot

3. an old wedge of lemon

4. a *very* old-looking potato

5. two string beans

Not exactly the perfect toppings for a prize-winning pizza.

Just then she heard a huge rumbling sound outside. She looked out the kitchen window just in time to see a massive truck lumbering down the street.

Bonnie sighed, and studied the rest of the contents of the refrigerator. She found: a hacked-at chunk of Swiss cheese, a small bowl of tuna, four slices of meat loaf, three-fourths of a diet lemon-meringue pie that tasted so soapy no one in the family would eat it. A can of olives—

Bonnie had seen enough! She slammed the refrigerator door. *"Mom,"* she yelled. "When are you going shopping?"

"Dad's doing it tonight on his way home from

work," her mother called back. "You can call him if you want to add something to—"

The roar of another passing truck drowned out the rest of her sentence.

"—the list." Mrs. Kirk's voice sounded much too loud in the sudden silence. "He'll be there until six or so, so you have another half hour."

But what was the use of calling him when Bonnie had no idea what she wanted him to buy?

"I'll just go over there later on my bike," Bonnie shouted. "Right now I've got to get over to school to get the lunchroom ready for to-morrow night."

VVVVVVVVRRRRRRROOOOOOOOOOO-OMMMMMMMMMMMM! went a third truck. In the cupboard the glasses all tinkled threat-eningly.

"Bye, Mom!" Bonnie called over all the rum-bling and tinkling. "I'll eat dinner when I get back!" Grabbing a jacket, she rushed out the back door.

As she walked down the block, Bonnie spot-ted Bob raking leaves in his front yard. Out of habit, she started to call out to him—but the instant Bob saw *her*, he threw down the rake and walked inside without a word.

Bonnie walked past him as briskly as she

could. She hoped he could hear what she was thinking, even though she knew he couldn't possibly. *I may have changed my pizza for you—even though you don't know it—but I'm doing just fine without you. I don't need you at all!*

Bonnie kept up a snappy pace all the way to school, just in case Bob was somehow watching her. As she strode along, she made a mental list of all the things she needed to do tonight.

Meet with Diego, she jotted down in her head. *Move the lunchroom tables. Decorate the walls. Set up the judges' stand. Make sure to—*

As she reached the Hollis parking lot, she suddenly stopped in her tracks.

"What are all those trucks doing there?" she asked aloud.

Four gigantic trucks were parked in the circle in front of the school. Workers were scuttling in and out of them, taking out dozens of wooden crates and piling them by the front door. The pile was growing bigger and bigger.

Those must have been the trucks I heard earlier, Bonnie thought. *Maybe it's the new cafeteria chairs or something. Wow, there sure are a lot of crates! I wonder where they're all—*

"Hey, Bonnie! What *is* all this stuff?" Bonnie

turned to see Jennifer and Tiffany walking toward her. "This guy says it's for you!" Jennifer added, pointing to a cheerful-looking man in jeans and a flannel shirt, standing by the school doors.

"Are you Bonnie Kirk?"

"Yes, I am."

"Great! Mr. Rock sent me. He said to make sure I talked to you."

"Mr. Rock?" Bonnie asked, puzzled.

"Oh, you know. That guy you talked to the other day, Chef what's-his-name?"

"Oh, Chef Roche! He sent you?"

"Yeah. Here's the stuff you wanted for your dance, or whatever it is." The man gestured toward the towering mound of crates.

"That's *all* for us?" Bonnie whispered.

"What's the matter? Isn't it enough?"

"*Enough!* All we needed were some pizza toppings. There must be enough to feed ten thousand people in those crates!"

"Gross," said Jennifer.

"Oh, no," said Tiffany.

"And more coming," the man in the flannel shirt said with satisfaction. "Guess that Mr. Rock really liked you. He called up all the chefs he knew and asked them to send you stuff, too."

Bonnie didn't answer. She couldn't. Silently,

she walked over and stared at the crates.

There was plenty of stuff to make pizza toppings with, that was for sure. The crates were crammed with every kind of food imaginable—cheeses and mushrooms and grapes and oranges and peppers and tomatoes and . . . It was enough to make you dizzy. There were vats of chocolate mousse and ice cream. There were hams and salamis and olive oil and onions. There were huge sacks of sunflower seeds and hundreds of loaves of French bread. There were quail eggs and hazelnuts and—

"Okay, I guess that's it!" the man in the flannel shirt said happily as the last panting workman dropped the last crate with a thud. "Enjoy!"

He hopped into the cab of the first truck and signaled to the rest of the drivers.

"Wait!" Bonnie called frantically. Tiffany let out a frightened scream. But they were both too late.

All four trucks roared to life and pulled away from the school, leaving the girls alone with enough food to feed the entire Hollis Elementary School for the next ten years, and no place to put it!

Chapter Eight

Countdown to Pizza Night

A couple of seconds after the four trucks lurched out of the school parking lot, a car pulled in.

"Oh, no!" Bonnie wailed. "It's Ms. Weinstock! How am I going to explain about all this food?"

Tiffany was practically in tears. "Oh, no," she moaned. "We're going to be arrested!"

"Don't be ridiculous!" snapped Jennifer. "You don't get arrested for having someone give you too much food! *They're* the ones who should get in trouble. I mean, think of all the temptation they're throwing at us! How am I supposed to stay on my diet when—"

"Oh, thank heaven! It's *not* Ms. Weinstock!" Bonnie interrupted.

For once, luck was on her side. It was Diego Lopez. He vaulted out of the car, waved good-bye to his father, and came loping up to the three girls.

"Hi! I see Ms. Weinstock's not here yet. Do you want me to pick the lock? Hey, what's all this food doing here?"

"This food," Bonnie said in despair, "is our pizza toppings for tomorrow night."

Tiffany gave a long, throbbing sniff.

"But that's great! Why do you guys look so . . ." Diego bent down and studied the crates more closely. "We're supposed to put *chocolate mousse* on our pizzas? What's the deal here?"

"I don't know!" Bonnie wailed. "I guess Chef Roche was trying to be nice! But if Ms. Weinstock sees all this stuff, she'll drop dead. She was worried about wasting the *pizzas*, remember? Now she'll have to worry about wasting nine million tons of good food!" Savagely, Bonnie kicked a crate that held containers of sour cream. "And most of it's not healthy, either," she groaned. "She'll never let us have it."

"Well, it's no biggie," said Diego. "All we have to do is pull out the stuff we can use. Chill out. I'll take care of it. . . . I'll just go through the crates and pull out anything that looks as though it could go on a pizza. Then I'll put the rest away somewhere."

"*Where?*" Jennifer asked him coldly. "Out on the football field?"

"I said I'd take care of it," Diego answered. His voice rose. "But if I were you, *I'd* try to think of a story to tell Ms. Weinstock fast. She's heading right this way."

Bonnie looked up. Ms. Weinstock's little blue car was rocketing toward the parking lot next to the school.

"Oh, no!"

"Oh, *yes*. C'mon, Bonnie! Quick! What should we tell her?"

"Yeah, Bonnie! What do we do now?" asked Jennifer.

"Bonnie? Bonnie? B-B-Bonnie!" Now Tiffany really did begin to cry.

Bonnie's brain was racing frantically. "She's parking in the parking lot instead of in front of the school. So she can't have noticed the crates yet. Let's tell her...let's tell her... we've got to stop her before she gets here."

"You're right!" Diego said. "We'll head her off at the pass. Maybe we can get her to go in by the side entrance."

"Hurry!" said Jennifer.

The four of them raced toward Ms. Weinstock's car. As she turned off the engine and opened the door, they hurled themselves at her.

"Hi, kids!" Ms. Weinstock said. "What's

the—*oof!*" Bonnie had just collided with her.

"Oh, Ms. Weinstock, I'm so glad you're here!" Bonnie gasped. "I saw smoke coming out of one of the first-grade classrooms!" The building's side entrance was in the first-grade wing.

"Oh, how terrible!" said Ms. Weinstock. She glanced around anxiously. "I'll run to that house over there"—she pointed to a little white house next to the playground—"and ask if I can call the fire department. You kids stay right here, now. I don't want you getting hurt!"

The four classmates stared at each other in dismay. Their plan wasn't working. More trucks? That was the last thing they needed.

"Well, maybe I didn't see any smoke," Bonnie said quickly. "I mean, maybe I just imagined it. Shouldn't we go in and make sure first?"

"We'd look pretty silly if the fire department got here and there was no fire," Diego put in.

"Yes, let's go in the side entrance," Tiffany begged her. "There's no sense in using the *front*!"

Naturally, that made Ms. Weinstock glance curiously over at the front door. "What are all those crates doing out there?" she asked.

"Well . . ." Tiffany began.

Bonnie gave her ankle a warning kick.

"I don't know," Tiffany finished.

"Look! There's the smoke again!" Jennifer cried, pointing over at the side entrance.

"Okay, we'll check it out," Ms. Weinstock agreed. "But *hurry!*"

The five of them rushed to the side entrance. Ms. Weinstock fumbled with the key. At last, she and the four kids burst through the side door into the darkened hallway of the first-grade wing.

Ms. Weinstock sniffed the air cautiously. "I don't smell smoke . . . ," she began.

"You can't always smell it!" Diego said firmly.

"He's right," Bonnie said in a quavery voice. "Come on!" She led Ms. Weinstock and the others past the closed doors of the classrooms and down the hallway walls lined with first-grade artwork. Then Bonnie stopped in front of a grayish-orange finger-painted blob with the title "My Daddy."

"I guess I was wrong about the fire," she said in what she hoped was a sheepish voice. "Sorry, Ms. Weinstock."

"Oh, that's all right, dear," said Ms. Weinstock. "It's always better to be careful about these things. Shall we head down to the lunchroom?"

"SURE!" Bonnie said, much too brightly. She gave Diego a look that said: "Help!" They couldn't keep Ms. Weinstock in the lunchroom forever. And they still had to find a place to hide those crates!

"Hey," Diego said as they got to the lunchroom door. "I better run to my locker. I think I heard something dripping in there when we passed it."

"Something *dripping*?" Ms. Weinstock asked.

"Oh, you know boys' lockers!" Bonnie said quickly. "They're full of all kinds of things! A nest of baby birds was once born in my brother's, and he never noticed until they learned how to fly."

"I didn't know you had a bro—" Tiffany began. "*Ouch!* Jennifer, why did you step on my foot?"

"Sorry," Jennifer said coolly. "I thought I saw a cockroach under it."

"I'll be right back!" Diego said.

In a couple of minutes he returned, looking incredibly dejected.

"It's a jar of honey," he said as if he could barely drag out the words. "It spilled all over my stuff. Ms. Weinstock, I hate not to be able to help you in the lunchroom, but would it be okay if I cleaned out my locker instead?"

"A jar of honey? Oh, dear, what a waste of good food!" Ms. Weinstock said. "Of course you should go clean it up. In fact, why don't the girls and I help you?"

"*No*," Diego yelled. "I mean, don't bother. It's—it's just too messy for anyone to see. I'll take care of it myself, and then I'll come back to help *you*."

"Do you think the judges should have glasses of water?" Ms. Weinstock asked a few minutes later. She and Bonnie were setting up the judges' table at one end of the lunchroom. "To cleanse their palates between bites?"

I think the judges will need industrial-strength mouthwash to get rid of the taste of some of these pizzas, Bonnie thought. But all she said out loud was, "Sure. That's a great idea."

As they walked toward the kitchen, Ms. Weinstock suddenly asked, "What is that horrible thumping sound I keep hearing? It sounds as though someone's dragging a trunk through the halls!"

"Must be Diego," Bonnie answered, correctly enough. She picked up three glasses and ran over the judges' table with them. "He's probably...uhhh...cleaning his books off, you know? What should we do next?"

Ms. Weinstock looked around the room. Jennifer was decorating the lunchroom windows with crepe-paper streamers. It was taking a long time, because she kept stopping to glance at her reflection in the glass. Tiffany was busily gluing sequins to cardboard to make another of her famous posters. This one said:

WELCOME TO THE NIGHT OF 1,000 PIZZAS
HELP YOURSELF TO TOPPINGS
BUT LEAVE ENOUGH FOR THE
NEXT PERSON!
AND BE CAREFUL NOT TO SLIP
ON THE FLOOR!

"It's hideous, isn't it?" she moaned when she saw Bonnie looking at the poster. "I think I should just start all over again!"

Bonnie rolled her eyes wearily. Didn't Tiffany ever get tired of that particular compliment-getting technique?

She shrugged. "It's okay," she said. "But why did you put in that last line?"

"Don't you think it's a good idea?" Tiffany asked anxiously. "I thought that with all these people and all this food, there might be some accidents! Someone could get hurt. But I'll cross it off if you don't like it. I'll just cross it off, even if it makes this poster look even worse than it does already."

"Never mind," said Bonnie. Before Tiffany could get her second wind, she turned to Ms. Weinstock. "What next?" she repeated.

"Let's color the waterfall!" Jennifer called from the window. She put down her streamers and walked over to them.

"Color the waterfall?" Ms. Weinstock asked.

"Yes—you know, dye it with food coloring. It would look so much nicer than just plain old transparent water, don't you think? I thought of it in the night, and I bought some red food coloring on the way here." Proudly, Jennifer held up a large bottle filled with brilliant red liquid.

"That's a lot of food coloring," Bonnie said.

"Seventy-five of those little plastic bottles," Jennifer replied proudly. "I bought two cases! Then I put them all together and filled up this whole quart bottle!"

"But Jennifer," said Ms. Weinstock, "don't you think a red waterfall would look a little . . . well, *unnatural*?"

"Oh, no! It'll be great!" said Jennifer. "Watch!"

Before they could stop her, she darted over to the waterfall and poured in the whole quart bottle.

The effect was certainly dramatic. In about three seconds, the ornamental waterfall went from a clear, laughing blue to a deep, sinister red. And now that it was red, the cheerful gurgling noise it made sounded a lot less cheerful.

Tiffany screamed when she saw it.

"Well, Jennifer," said Ms. Weinstock after a second of helpless silence, "that certainly looks very *striking*."

"It looks like someone got murdered," Tiffany said, shivering.

"Maybe we can pretend it's tomato sauce," Bonnie said. "Do you want to dye anything *else*, Jennifer?"

"Uh—no," said Ms. Weinstock quickly. "As much as I admire . . . er . . . Jennifer's work, why don't we do something a little less . . . dramatic this time? How about replacing the foods in the vending machines?"

"Oh, are you getting rid of the old stuff?" Bonnie asked joyfully. "Hooray," said Jennifer. Even Tiffany cracked a smile. No more Herbal Medley or Celery–Carrot Joy. What a relief!

"You almost sound as if you *want* me to get

rid of it," Ms. Weinstock said in surprise. "These are wonderfully healthy foods. Don't you like them?"

Bonnie glanced at Jennifer and Tiffany. *Uh-oh*, she thought. *They're not going to be much help.* She took a deep breath and plunged in.

"Well, not exactly, Ms. Weinstock. I mean, they are healthy. Very healthy. But, well, you see, things like Herbal Medley just aren't what kids like to eat. They may be healthy, but they're just . . . just—"

"Horrible!" Tiffany supplied. Then she blushed. "I—I didn't really mean that, Ms. Weinstock," she stammered. "I don't know what came over me."

"I was wondering why none of the foods in the vending machines ever seemed to run out," said Ms. Weinstock slowly. "Are they really so bad?"

All three girls nodded.

"Sorry," Bonnie said, "but they really, really are. They're . . . well, I guess they're just too hard-core nutritious for us. Ms. Weinstock, aren't there *any* good-for-us foods that actually taste good?"

Ms. Weinstock paused. "Well, dried fruits are good for people," she said. "Raisins and dried apricots and—"

"That's just the kind of thing I mean!" said Bonnie enthusiastically. "And what about yogurt? Can't you put yogurt in a vending machine?"

"As long as it wouldn't spill," put in Tiffany.

"Sure I could," said Ms. Weinstock. "I tell you what, girls. As soon as Pizza Night is over, I'll get together with anyone who's interested, and we'll talk about finding some foods we can *all* live with."

"Sounds great," said Bonnie, and she meant it. "Now, is there anything more we can do to get ready? Because if there isn't, I should probably get home and work on my pizza idea."

Ms. Weinstock looked around the room. "That crepe paper! Those posters! It's perfect," she told Bonnie, Tiffany, and Jennifer. "It's a pizza paradise: Night of a Thousand Pizzas! You've done an *exceptional* job, girls! I'm sure Diego will be just *heartbroken* that he couldn't help out. No, I think we're all done here. All we need to do is wait until tomorrow night."

Chapter Nine

On Your Mark,
Get Set...

"THE NIGHT OF A THOUSAND PIZZAS IS OFFICIALLY OPEN!" boomed Mr. Haypence. With a grand, sweeping motion, he cut the ribbon at the door to the lunchroom, and what looked like a tidal wave of contestants rushed in.

"Oh, Bonnie!" Tiffany moaned. "I just know there aren't going to be enough pizzas to go around! It's going to be a disaster!"

For once, Bonnie was as worried as Tiffany. She had never seen so many people in her life. Or maybe she had—at Disneyland and places like that—but she had never seen so many of them in one elementary-school lunchroom before. It looked as though the whole town of Pasadena had decided that a pizza contest was the perfect activity for a Thursday night. There was even a television crew from the local news wandering around and getting into everyone's way.

Mr. Haypence was busy strolling through the crowds, looking as proud as if he'd organized the whole event himself. Every time he came anywhere near the range of the TV crew's camera, he straightened his tie and his wide smile grew even wider. Ms. Weinstock was darting from place to place on vague little errands—straightening the water glasses on the judges' table, polishing the chrome on the vending machines. In the kitchen, Bonnie could see the lunch ladies frantically handing out all the leftover frozen pizzas. There was a huge line of people waiting, and as soon as each pizza was pulled out of the freezer, someone snatched it and rushed off with it.

Another huge line of people had formed at the tables of toppings that Diego had set up that afternoon. Bonnie had asked him if he wanted any help, but he had said no.

"I can fix it up myself," he told her. "You just stay at home and work on your pizza, Bonnie."

Looking at the tables now, Bonnie had to admit Diego had done a great job. There was everything you could possibly want to put on a pizza there and more, everything from olives to sirloin tips. All top-quality ingredients, too. The kids in Mrs. Doubleday's class might have gotten a head start on their own pizzas, but the general public was going to be able to put up some pretty stiff competition.

"Would you *mind* getting out of the way?" a voice behind Bonnie asked coldly. "Some of us are trying to get in line here."

Bonnie turned. It was Bob. His arms were folded, and he was tapping his foot impatiently. He looked so cranky that Bonnie found herself mirroring his bad mood.

"*Why* are some of us trying to get in line?" she asked Bob in a voice that was dripping with false sweetness. "Didn't some of us have *time* to get our pizzas ready at home?"

"There was a little accident on the way to school! All right?" Bob snapped. "I dropped my tomato sauce, and it spilled over the rest of my ingredients. Now are you satisfied?"

"Oh, perfectly," said Bonnie. She stepped back and let Bob step into line.

"I suppose your Pizza Classico is going to win the contest?" Bob asked grimly.

"As a matter of fact, I came up with a much, much better idea than that," Bonnie replied crossly. "*Not* that I'm going to let you know what it is. You'd probably steal it right out from under my nose."

Bob shrugged. "Was the red waterfall *your* idea, by the way?" he asked after a pause. "It looks really lovely, Bonnie. The Cascade of Blood—so suitable for family entertainment!"

"Uhh . . . it was Jennifer's idea," Bonnie said stiffly, "and I think it looks very nice. Very— uh—festive."

"Well, that's one word for it."

"No, no, no, no, *no*, honey!" a woman next to them told her little boy. "G.I. Joes won't be *good* on a pizza!"

"Mommy, my G.I. Joes *want* to go on the pizza!" he wailed.

"But, Roger, you don't want them to go into the oven, do you?" asked the little boy's mother. "They'll melt!"

Roger thought about that for a second. "Oh, okay," he said at last. "I'll use my racing cars instead."

"May I have your attention, please?" came Mr. Haypence's voice from the microphone on the stage. "I'd like to introduce our three judges for this evening. A big hand for Mrs. Dowdy, Mr. Windle, and Mrs. Carlson!"

There was a roar of enthusiastic applause. Mrs. Dowdy bowed proudly and low, like an opera singer. The home-ec teacher actually had gone ahead and made herself a long black judge's robe. But somehow the robe—which was about a foot too long—wasn't quite as impressive-looking as Mrs. Dowdy had probably intended.

Mr. Windle didn't bow. Instead he stepped up to the microphone, to Mr. Haypence's obvious surprise. "I'm delighted to...," he said. "It's nice to see such a large...Doesn't that pizza smell..." Then Mr. Haypence grabbed the microphone away from him.

Mrs. Carlson just waved and smiled. "Let's get going!" she said cheerfully. "I can't wait to try those pizzas!"

"We will, we will," said Mr. Haypence, "but first I want to introduce our hostess for the evening. Ms. Weinstock, will you please explain the rules of the contest?"

Ms. Weinstock walked slowly up the steps. She looked almost as pale as she had on the first day of school.

She picked up the microphone and cleared her throat. "THE JUDGES," she blared out in a startlingly loud voice. Everyone gasped, and Mr. Haypence dashed forward and adjusted the microphone.

"You have one half-hour to prepare your pizzas," Ms. Weinstock went on in her normal voice. "Please describe your recipe briefly on the index cards we'll be passing out in a minute. The judges will sample one slice of pizza from each entry. Entries will be judged on taste, originality, *and nutritional content*," she finished firmly. From somewhere in the audience, Rocky Latizano gave a loud disappointed groan. "There will be a first, second, and third prize, plus three honorable mentions. After the judging, all the pizzas may be eaten. Soft drinks will be available, and of course, fresh fruit juices," Ms. Weinstock finished.

Then Mr. Haypence stepped forward again. "Are there any questions?"

"What are the prizes?" someone called out.

"Handsome, well-made ribbons in very attractive shades," Mr. Haypence answered. There were groans from the audience. Everyone was disappointed.

And then Ms. Weinstock stepped up to the microphone again. "But the winning pizza *will* be added to our regular lunchroom menu," she said quickly. "And it will be named after whoever wins the contest. So at least the winner will become part of Hollis history."

"Any other questions?" asked Mr. Haypence. "No? Then LET THE PIZZAS BEGIN!"

* * *

Most of the kids in Mrs. Doubleday's class were all working in one corner of the lunchroom. Bonnie's pizza was done so quickly that she decided to spend the rest of the half-hour watching her classmates work on theirs.

Except for Bob. He was working on his pizza across the room, and whenever Bonnie caught his eye he flung himself around to shield his pizza from her view. Bonnie could hardly believe he was acting like such a baby. *How could I tell what's in his stupid pizza from across the room anyway?* The first pizza she noticed was Rocky Latizano's. The more closely she looked, the more queasy she felt, but it was too late to escape. Rocky had seen her.

"Hey, come take a look!" he called enthusiastically. "Whaddya think?"

"What is this, exactly?" Bonnie said, sidestepping his question.

"Oh, the same pizza I showed you before, with a couple of changes," Rocky told her. "Here. You can read my card. See, I took your advice!"

He held out an index card that was so oily it was transparent. On it he had written "ROCKY'S PIZZA-FRY—because everyone loves fried food *and* pizza. Topped with fried chicken, fried clams, bacon bits, crushed potato chips, and fried zucchini. Eat hearty!"

"See, I added the clams and the zucchini to make it healthier," Rocky added proudly. "Wasn't that smart?"

Bonnie just looked at him. "It was very smart, Rocky," she said.

"What are you making?" Rocky asked.

"Oh, just some kind of odds and ends," Bonnie told him evasively. "It's kind of hard to describe."

Jennifer's pizza was nowhere near done. That's because she was still fussing over how the pink candy hearts she had brought from home should be arranged on top.

"They've got to be just right!" she fretted. "What do you think, Bonnie? Is this pretty enough?"

"It looks very pretty," Bonnie said, glancing at the pink and blue ribbons, sequins, and hearts Jennifer had arranged on her pizza. "But I don't think Ms. Weinstock said anything about judging the pizzas by the way they look. Maybe you should leave the hearts for now and think about putting some *real* food on top first."

Jennifer frowned. "Get real! I *can't* put the food on until I know where the decorations are going to be!"

"Want to buy a slice of the winning pizza, girls?" said Junior Smith. "I'm preselling them."

"What do you mean, preselling?" Bonnie asked.

He grinned—a perfect salesman's grin. "Well, I'll let you in on a little secret," he said. "I know I'm going to win this contest. Once my pizza wins, everyone's going to want some. But I'd have to be crazy just to *give* it away, wouldn't I? So I'm letting people invest in some of Pasadena's best pizza now, at the prewinning price. Once I win, of course, the price is going to go *way*, *way* up. Hey, that's a great name, isn't it . . . Pasadena's Best Pizza? Maybe I'll open a chain! And that's all the *more* reason why you should invest in my pizza!"

"Hang on a sec," said Bonnie. "Before I buy any, why are you so sure you're going to win?"

"Why? Because I've got the classiest pizza in this room! Look at what's on top of this baby!" Junior boasted. "Caviar, pâté, lobster, crab claws . . ."

"Junior, did you buy all that stuff?" asked Bonnie. Somehow she couldn't see him spending that much money, even for a presold pizza.

"Are you kidding?" Junior replied. "It's all foods that my parents have gotten in gift baskets over the years. Now, come on, tell me—have you ever seen a more expensive-looking pizza?"

"Well, no," Bonnie said. "But somehow I just don't think I can afford even one slice."

"Me either," said Jennifer. "Besides, I'm saving all my money to buy a home-tanning kit."

Diego was scanning a computer printout so intently that Bonnie didn't dare interrupt him. "Computer-generated Pizza," said the title on his index card—but the description he'd written was so complicated that Bonnie couldn't get past the first couple of words.

But Tiffany was all too eager to talk to Bonnie. "This is a *terrible* pizza, isn't it?" she said. "Don't you think I should just start over?"

I've had it, thought Bonnie. *She's done this to me one too many times*.

"Well, as a matter of fact—" Bonnie began. Then she stopped in midsentence with a worried expression on her face.

"You *do* think I should!" Tiffany asked. "Bonnie, I thought you were my friend! Anyway, this pizza is just fine! Why should I start over?"

Bonnie left her sputtering and walked over to the Watson twins' table. The two pizzas the twins were working on were the ugliest, messiest excuses for pizza she had ever seen. It looked as though the twins had ransacked every cupboard in their house and every garbage can on their block to come up with the ingredients.

"What kind of pizza *is* that?" Bonnie asked Louie Watson.

"Well, mine's called Everything but the Kitchen Sink," he said proudly. "And Larry's is called Everything but the Bathroom Sink. Let's see, Lar, what did we put in these exactly?"

"Uh, that's okay," said Bonnie. "I don't think I really want to—"

"YOUR TIME IS UP!" came Mr. Haypence's voice over the microphone.

Startled, Larry Watson jumped to his feet. As he did so, he banged into the table. Both pizzas flew into the air and smacked each other in the face—if a pizza has a face. They landed back on the table, sandwiched together in a messy heap.

"Oh, well," said Louie philosophically. "Let's just pull 'em apart again. It won't make any difference. Hey, they're stuck together!"

I'd better get back to my table, thought Bonnie. *The Human Demolition Team strikes again. This is one thing I* don't *want to watch.*

As she hurried back to her place, she heard Jennifer wailing, "But I haven't even put the *food* on my pizza yet!"

Chapter Ten

And the Winner Is...

Slowly, slowly, and more slowly still, the three judges moved from table to table. Their shoulders were slumped, their heads bowed. Their hands moved sluggishly across their pads as they took notes, and they chewed as if their jaws ached.

The three of them had been judging for two hours. They'd checked out most of the entries. And they had *definitely* had enough pizza. True, they'd sampled only a few bites from each entry—but there were more than six hundred pizzas in the room.

"How many whole pizzas do you think they've each had?" Bonnie heard Bob asking Diego.

"I don't *want* to think about it," Diego answered.

"Could you bring us some more water,

please?" Mrs. Dowdy asked Bonnie in a faint voice.

"Yes, that would be most..." Mr. Windle chimed in. "It would help to make things a little..."

"Easier?" Bonnie asked. He nodded firmly.

"Chins up," Mrs. Carlson said encouragingly. "There are only a few more."

By this time the judges had finished with most of the kids in Mrs. Doubleday's class. They were coming up to Rocky's Pizza-Fry now—and Bonnie thought she had never seen such looks of horror on anyone's face as she did on the judges' when Mrs. Carlson read Rocky's description out loud.

"I don't think I need to try this," Mrs. Dowdy said. "It looks wonderful," she told Rocky quickly, "but your description is so—so vivid that it conveys the whole spirit of the pizza all by itself."

The other two judges took mouse-sized bites, and Bonnie thought she heard Mr. Windle groaning faintly as he turned away to write down his opinion.

"Great!" said Rocky with satisfaction. "That means there's more for me!"

If the judges had looked horrified when they came to Rocky's pizza, they looked absolutely stricken when they came to the two pizzas of the Watson twins.

For a minute and a half (Bonnie was watching the wall clock), the judges stood silently gazing at the two piles of wreckage that were the boy's pizzas. *I guess the twins* did *manage to pry them apart,* Bonnie thought with a shudder. Then Mr. Windle picked up Larry's description card.

"'Everything but the...,'" he read aloud. Quickly he put down the card and picked up Louie's. "'Everything but the...,'" he read again. He looked helplessly at his two colleagues. "Well, shall we..."

"You know, I think we can probably judge these pizzas by sight," said Mrs. Dowdy. "We don't really need to try them." She smiled thinly at the two boys. "After all, I'm sure you can understand that we'd feel much too uncomfortable if we had to eat *every* pizza in this room!"

Mr. Windle nodded gratefully, and even Mrs. Carlson didn't disagree.

"Hey, no fair!" bellowed Larry. "You have to try ours!"

Both twins burst into a volley of shouts.

"I'm suing!"

"Unfair!"

"You're a bunch of cowards!"

"No taxation without representation!" (Mrs. Doubleday's class was studying the American Revolution.)

In a matter of seconds, Mr. Haypence had wafted across the room. The television crew was right behind him.

"Is there some kind of problem, boys?" Mr. Haypence asked suavely.

"Oh, no!" said Mrs. Dowdy instantly. "We're all very excited at the prospect of tasting these—uh—pizzas here!" She picked up a slice of Everything But the Kitchen Sink, closed her eyes, and took a bite.

Her eyes flew open in surprise. "This is actually quite good!" she said to Mrs. Carlson and Mr. Windle. "Try some!"

Staring at her in disbelief, both judges did. And both of them had the same reaction she'd had. "Let's try the...," Mr. Windle said eagerly, reaching for a slab of Everything But the Bathroom Sink.

Once again, all three judges were delighted. "Unusual but delicious," Bonnie heard Mrs. Dowdy murmuring as she jotted down her reaction. "Has that indefinable...," Mr. Windle said as he scribbled down his notes.

And Mrs. Carlson wrote, "Whatever they put in these, it works!"

The judges were looking much more cheerful as they approached Bob's table. Bonnie couldn't see what he had made, but the judges seemed to like it too—although they didn't jump for joy the way they had at the Watsons' table.

"Let's see, is anyone left?" Mrs. Dowdy asked. "I think we may be all—"

"Just a minute," Bonnie heard herself saying. "You haven't tried mine yet."

Was it her imagination, or did all three judges seem to sigh as they moved toward her?

Mrs. Dowdy picked up Bonnie's card. " 'Leftover Night,' " she said, and she began to read what Bonnie had finished writing that afternoon.

" 'Since most families don't have lots of exciting ingredients in their refrigerators, I have decided to make my pizza out of the most commonly found leftovers in the average household. My pizza has leftover tuna, leftover peas, leftover—' "

To Bonnie's astonishment, Mrs. Dowdy stopped reading and set the card down with a snap. "There seems to be a little problem here, Bonnie," she said coldly. "What is the explanation for the fact that you and Bob Kelly have chosen identical ideas for your pizzas?"

Mrs. Dowdy strode back to Bob's table and picked up his card. " 'The Day-After Pizza,' " she read aloud. " 'It's not easy making leftovers taste good, and it's even harder making leftovers taste good on a pizza. But I have tried to—' "

"What?" Bonnie shrieked. She turned to Bob, who was staring openmouthed at her. "Bob Kelly, you copied me!" she shouted.

"I copied *you!"* he yelled back. "You're the one who copied *me!"*

"How could I have done that?" Bonnie snapped. "My pizza was all ready to be put together when I got here! *You're* the one who came to school without having a pizza ready!"

"I . . . you're right," Bob said slowly. "But I didn't copy you, Bonnie."

He cleared his throat. "I wasn't exactly telling the truth when I said I'd dropped my tomato sauce on the way here. What really happened was that I decided not to do my Traditional Pizza. I wanted you to have a better chance with yours. So I had to wing it when I got here—and since the only things left on the table were sort of moth-eaten, I decided they looked like leftovers. That's all," he finished simply.

"I can't believe this!" Bonnie gasped. "I decided to change *my* idea so that you'd have a better chance with *your* pizza! And the only things *we* had in the house were leftovers!"

She and Bob stared at each other in silence. Then—at the same time—they both broke into grins.

"It was just a coincidence, Mrs. Dowdy," Bonnie said lightly.

All three judges were smiling now, too. "Well, isn't that a . . ." Mr. Windle said. "Shall we try the . . ."

"It's good, Bonnie," said Mrs. Carlson politely after they'd all tried Leftover Night. "I'm not sure it's going to win the first prize, but—"

"Oh, I don't care whether it wins or not," said Bonnie. *I'm just glad all the fighting's over*, she added to herself.

Neither Bob's nor Bonnie's pizza won first prize, but they did win a combined honorable mention for best coincidence.

Another honorable mention—for originality—went to the little boy who had put G.I. Joes on his pizza. "I guess he got his own way after all," Bonnie said to Bob. "It just shows that you should never do what your parents tell you to." And a third honorable mention went to Diego Lopez.

"I'm sure glad I figured out what that print-out said," he told everyone as he bounded up the stairs to get his ribbon.

Third prize went to a family with five children who had been squabbling with each other the whole time they'd been working on their Tex-Mex Pizza. They were still arguing and grabbing the third prize ribbon from one another as they left the stage.

Second prize also went to someone who didn't go to Hollis—a jolly-looking older woman who had made a pizza shaped like a gingerbread boy.

And first prize?

Mr. Haypence finished shaking hands with the second-prize winner and stepped up to the microphone again.

"I'm sure we're all waiting to hear who won first prize," he said, stretching his lips into a smile so wide it could have swallowed the TV camera before him. "And I think it's safe to say that this prize comes as a big, big surprise to all of us."

"Get on with it!" shouted Rocky Latizano.

Mr. Haypence glared in Rocky's direction. "The first prize is a surprise tie," he went on. "And the surprise is that the two pizzas that won it are those two disgusting-looking... I mean, those two unique pizza arrangements made by none other than Hollis's own Watson twins! Let's give them a big hand!"

"I don't believe it!" Junior Smith said bitterly. "They passed up on the classiest pizza in the world and the chance to make millions for that *mess*!"

Rocky Latizano just looked puzzled. "I don't get it!" he said. "I made my pizza healthy and everything! Maybe I should have used onion rings instead of fried zucchini...or fried shrimp instead of fried clams?" He picked up a huge, greasy slab of Rocky's Pizza-Fry and took a thoughtful bite.

"Tastes great to me," he said thickly. "I guess those judges just don't know a good thing when they see it."

Jennifer Stevens clicked her tongue impatiently. "I *know* I could have won if they'd just given me a little more time," she said.

And Tiffany Root burst into tears. "You should have let me start over!" she wailed at Bonnie. "I *knew* my pizza was terrible!"

Of course, the Watson twins were too overjoyed to listen to any of this. Red-faced and beaming, they scrambled up the steps to the stage.

It wasn't really either of their faults that

Larry tripped over the microphone and accidentally snapped it in two, or that Louie shook hands with the judges so vigorously that he flipped Mrs. Dowdy off the stage by mistake.

When the last pizza had been eaten—or, in the case of some of the pizzas, not even touched—and Mrs. Dowdy had untangled herself from her judge's robe, Ms. Weinstock walked onto the stage again. The lunchroom fell silent as she held up her hand.

"I'd like to thank everyone for making this evening such a success," she said. "Bonnie, Mr. Haypence, Diego, our wonderful cafeteria staff, Tiffany, Jennifer... Could you all come up on stage with me, please?"

There was a burst of applause as everyone who had worked on Pizza Night filed up the steps and stood close together at the edge of the stage.

"Let's open the curtain," Ms. Weinstock said. "There's really not enough room for all of us in front of it."

"No, don't!" Diego yelled—just seconds too late. Ms. Weinstock had already run to the side of the stage and whisked the curtain open.

Behind the curtain were all the crates of

food that *hadn't* been made into pizzas. And— how was it possible?—there seemed to be even more of them than there had been in front of the school yesterday. Next to the huge mound of crates, Ms. Weinstock looked about the size of a Barbie doll.

"Chocolate mousse," she read aloud in a shocked voice, staring at the nearest crate. "Ruby grapefruits. Wild boar bacon. Corn on the cob. Wild rice. Crown roast of— Can somebody please tell me what this *is*?"

"You said you were going to take care of those crates!" Bonnie hissed furiously at Diego.

"Well, I *did* take care of them!" he hissed back. "I didn't say I was going to solve the problem!"

Ms. Weinstock turned to face the lunchroom again. "Can anyone tell me what we're supposed to do with all this food?" she asked wonderingly.

Slowly Bonnie raised her hand.

"Yes, Bonnie?"

Bonnie glanced over at Bob. He was giving her a warning look, she could tell. She knew what that look meant as clearly as if she'd heard him say the words: *Shut up, Bonnie!*

Don't say a word! But Bonnie couldn't help herself.

"Yes, Bonnie?" Ms. Weinstock said faintly.

Bonnie cleared her throat. "How about a Night of a Thousand Toppings?"